FREE RUNNER

FREE RUNNER

DAVID TRIFUNOV

James Lorimer & Company Ltd., Publishers
Toronto

James Lorimer & Company Ltd., Publishers acknowledges funding support from the Ontario Arts Council (OAC), an agency of the Government of Ontario. We acknowledge the support of the Canada Council for the Arts, which last year invested $153 million to bring the arts to Canadians throughout the country. This project has been made possible in part by the Government of Canada and with the support of the Ontario Media Development Corporation.

Cover design: Shabnam Safari
Cover image: iStock

Library and Archives Canada Cataloguing in Publication

Trifunov, David, author
    Freerunner / David Trifunov.

(Sports stories)
Issued in print and electronic formats.
ISBN 978-1-4594-1280-4 (softcover).--ISBN 978-1-4594-1281-1 (EPUB)

    I. Title. II. Series: Sports stories (Toronto, Ont.)

PS8639.R535F73 2018   jC813'.6   C2017-906491-6
                                               C2017-906492-4

Published by: Distributed in Canada by: Distributed in the US by:
James Lorimer &   Formac Lorimer Books   Lerner Publisher Services
Company Ltd., Publishers   5502 Atlantic Street   1251 Washington Ave. N.
117 Peter Street, Suite 304 Halifax, NS, Canada   Minneapolis, MN, USA
Toronto, ON, Canada   B3H 1G4   55401
M5V 0M3   www.lernerbooks.com
www.lorimer.ca

Printed and bound in Canada.
Manufactured by Friesens Corporation in Altona, Manitoba,
Canada in December 2017.
Job # 239694

For my parents, Rick and Kathleen.

Contents

1 MALL MAYHEM

I laughed when I saw them — noise-cancelling headphones. I stole them anyway.

Well, not right away.

Aren't headphones supposed to be noisy? I thought as I scanned the box.

I had only been in Ottawa for a month. I didn't like it. The Rideau Centre mall was surrounded by homeless people. But it was filled with people who had too many homes: condos, cottages and vacation homes. I had no idea whether I belonged inside or outside. A woman's sleeve brushed my roughed up army surplus jacket as she headed for the checkout. All I could smell was flowery perfume. That scent probably cost more than what my mom spends on groceries in a month. Behind the woman was a girl about my age, maybe fourteen. Her tennis shoes were bright white and had sleek pink logos on the sides. She was carrying some kind of new tablet. Her lips were tight, like she was trying to hide a satisfied smile.

I headed for the escalator. I know now I should have kept going. I couldn't let it go, though. I reached the bottom, turned around and took the escalator right back up again. I walked back into the store and headed for the headphones.

That girl's mom was paying for the tablet. Since the cashier was trying to sell her junk she didn't need, I grabbed the headphones off the shelf. In a dark, deserted corner of the store, I ripped open the box and let the headphones drop into the saddle bag hanging near my hip. I walked through the security gates at the front of the store, expecting alarms. But nothing happened. I finally breathed.

I looked at the escalator crawling down. I'd be a sitting duck on it, so I walked through a door into the parking garage. As the door slammed shut, I collapsed against the wall. I put my hand on the bag to feel if the headphones were really there. They were.

All I could smell was exhaust. It didn't smell like freedom, so I forced myself to stand up again. I walked down the ramp toward the street. As I reached the sidewalk, the sun hit me and blinded me. I panicked. I couldn't see anything. I was convinced security guards would be waiting. The girl with the tablet and her mother would probably be there too. And they'd watch security lead me away.

My eyes adjusted. The street was empty.

You're such a baby sometimes, I thought.

I decided to walk toward the front of the mall and head into downtown. Maybe I could sell the headphones at a pawn shop. Then I thought about wearing them to school. They might keep people from talking to me. Who cares if I didn't have anything to plug them into? People would think they were wireless.

That's when my luck started to change — for the worse.

The number 97 bus to Bayshore left me in a cloud of blue smoke. It meant I'd have to find something to do for a half hour until the next one came. I looked at the mall. No way I could have gone back inside. The other day I'd noticed a pawn shop a couple of blocks away. Maybe someone there would want to buy the headphones.

"Hey, can you come with me?"

I didn't know the voice was talking to me at first. Then I felt someone touching my arm. I jumped and looked down. There was a hand on my wrist. I followed the hand to an arm under a long-sleeved blue shirt to a darker blue vest. On the vest were a walkie-talkie and a name tag. On the opposite side was a badge. Above the vest was a man's face. Dark skin and sunglasses.

I broke the hold on my wrist and ran.

Holy, I'm running from the police, I thought.

I turned back the way I came. Now the parking garage seemed like a safe place. There'd be lots of cars to hide between. Maybe I could climb into the bed of a pickup truck. Maybe there would be boxes or garbage bags I could hide under until the owner came back and drove out of there.

"Stop!"

The police officer sounded close. I skipped past the parking garage and bolted across the street.

A blue construction fence cut me off from some high-rise buildings. I jumped and caught the steel mesh. My fingers ached and my toes nearly slipped from the tiny metal holes. An entire block of fencing nearly toppled under me.

I found some grip and jumped again over top of it. I looked behind me. The cop had to find a longer way around. That fence bought me two more seconds to get away.

I turned another corner. The art gallery was across the street.

I sprinted in front of a line of cars turning left. The lead car hit the brakes, hard. Someone behind him honked. I caught a quick glimpse of the driver. She was staring at something behind me. I knew it was the cop.

I jumped for the gallery's fence. It was stone on the bottom. But the old metal spikes up top would do damage if I slipped. I grabbed the top of the corner pillar, put my foot on one of the spikes and jumped for the grass on the other side. It was awesome. It was like I was flying. But my plan backfired.

The cop just followed along the other side of the fence. He never tried to jump it. We even made eye contact. He was just waiting until we hit the break in the fence. He would just grab me.

If I was going to get out of there I had to keep taking risks.

Next was a handrail. I could jump that too. I grabbed the bar and swung my legs over the side.

I ran down a staircase back to the street. The cop was almost on top of me. I had one last chance to clear more construction fences and two of those giant garbage bins. Then I'd have to sprint through a construction site.

Thankfully the garbage bin was closed. I pushed off the top of it and jumped the fence.

I surprised a construction worker as I landed. I had to scramble over a pile of loose rock.

"Hey, get out of here," she yelled. "You're going to kill yourself."

Maybe she was right. But I would rather risk a police chase through a construction site than answer to my mother on a shoplifting charge.

Those rocks were my third strike.

The pile of rocks was deeper than I had thought. My footing gave out. I sprawled onto my face.

I could hear honking horns coming from a row of taxis parked outside the gallery. The drivers were whistling and cheering — for the cop.

"Phew! That was awesome," the cop said as he towered over me. "Kid, you can move! I thought you had me. But it looks like I have you, doesn't it?"

2 IT'S TRICKY

It was bad enough having a mall worker watching me like I was a criminal. But worse was her gum chewing. It was so loud I wanted to scream. Finally she stopped smacking her lips. The relative silence made the buzzing of the overhead lights sound like music. But she was still chewing. I wanted to say, "Don't you know how awful that sounds? You look like a cow when you do that." But I just stared at her, hoping she could read my mind and stop.

She didn't stop. All I could do was wait for the police to come back — with my mom. The cop had hauled me back to the mall's security office. They sat me down and asked me all kinds of questions. I had to tell them my mom's phone number at work. It was that or be taken to the police station.

I had to think about the better choice. Mall security or the police station? Mom was going to lose her mind either way. She had told me a thousand times why she moved us from Red Rock. It was so she could get a better job and I could have more opportunities.

Now, here I was. Just a few days at a new school in a new city and I'm caught shoplifting. Mom had to leave work early. She had to drive downtown. I know she hates driving downtown. After spending all her life in small-town Ontario, Ottawa might as well have been Los Angeles or New York City.

I knew it was going to be bad. So I couldn't figure out why Mom was laughing when the door opened.

"Just because I'm laughing, Patrick, doesn't mean I'm happy," she said.

I had always guessed she could read my mind. Now I knew it. I also knew she was serious. She only called me Patrick when she was serious.

The cop was laughing too. *Only five minutes together and they've teamed up against me,* I thought. I had no chance.

The cop sat down in one chair. Mom sat beside me.

"You can leave now," the cop said to the mall worker.

I studied the cop's vest. His name tag said, "Jack." He was huge. I thought he was going to break the chair just by sitting in it. How could a guy that big move fast enough to catch me?

He stuck out a meaty hand. "My name is Constable Ishman Jack. It's nice to meet you, Patrick."

We shook hands. Well, his hand swallowed mine. His grip was like iron.

Ishman, that's a weird name, I thought.

I didn't say that. "It's Tricky," I said.

"What is?"

"My name. Everybody calls me Tricky."

"He was always running away from me," Mom added. "Or slipping out of his crib."

It seemed more than a little strange to be talking like this. *Why are we all trying to make friends?* I didn't understand.

"Your mom says that breaking the law is not like you, Tricky. So I've got a deal to offer," the officer said. "The store won't press charges — and they really want to — if you do something for me. I've checked it out with your mom. She loves the idea."

Oh, no, I thought. *I'm going to be sweeping the streets for years.*

Both of them could tell I was getting nervous. It made my mom smile and laugh. She enjoyed watching me squirm.

"Have you ever heard of parkour?" the cop asked.

It didn't sound like an ancient torture device. I was somewhat relieved.

"Park? What?"

"Parkour. It comes from a French word that means 'journey.' But it's a sport too. What you did today outside the mall, that's kind of it. You see something in front of you — like fences or walls. And you get past them the fastest, best way you can."

I was still confused.

"It's like sport meets art," he continued. "It's the art of getting from one place to another in the most efficient way."

I still didn't understand. "So . . ."

The cop shifted his chair a little closer to mine. He actually cast a shadow over me. The world was closing in.

He pulled out his phone. "You like James Bond?"

My growing confusion must have shown on my face.

"The movies. You like his movies?" he prompted.

"Yeah, I guess."

He pulled up a video, a movie clip. Two guys were chasing each other through a construction site. People were running all over the place as stuff blew up around them. It was totally cool. But what did it have to do with me?

"That's parkour," he said.

"So you want me to be a stuntman?"

The cop laughed. My mom laughed. Of course they laughed. They were best friends.

"Sorry," he said, "not a stuntman. Parkour is like gymnastics and martial arts and obstacle course racing. I volunteer at a gym called Ground Zero. We teach parkour. If you promise to spend twelve weeks with me learning parkour, the store won't press charges."

The room went quiet again. The buzzing lights got louder. At least nobody was chewing gum.

"Say 'yes,'" Mom said. "It will make the car ride home a little happier."

It didn't sound right. That's all I had to do? Take some silly classes?

"So I just have to go to the gym?"

"Well, you have to try," said the cop. "I think you're going to like it. And I think you will be good at it. The gym is full of good people. Your mom agrees that it will be nice for you to make friends. You've just started grade nine, right? That's not easy in a new city."

I looked at Mom and frowned a little. She was still smiling at me. She had always been a happy person. But now she was freaking me out.

"I'm smiling like this because you got lucky, Tricky," Mom said. "Constable Jack wants to help you. Outside this office I was crying. In the car, driving over here, I was crying. Don't make me cry more, Patrick."

"It's one class per week for about an hour," the cop said. "If you want to come more often, or stay later, that's fine. After twelve weeks, you're a free man. Well, you're a free man everywhere but here. Mall security has your picture. They don't want you back here."

Of course I was going to say yes. What were my options? But I hated when people told me where to be, and at what time. Really, I wanted to move back home. I could live with my grandma in Thunder Bay or something.

I didn't say that. All I could manage was: "Okay."

3 WELCOME TO GROUND ZERO

It was Monday, the first day of my "punishment." Mom said I should call it "fun-ishment." I didn't laugh. I had spent some time watching parkour videos, and some of it looked cool. But I still couldn't understand why people did it.

I jumped on the bus after school and arrived at the gym twenty minutes later. I had nothing to do after school anyway. But it didn't mean I was excited about parkour.

At first I was sure I had the wrong address. When I stepped off the bus, I saw nothing but warehouses. A row of what looked like police cars were lined up outside some place called SureSecure. Next to it was what looked like an abandoned building with graffiti above the door. When I got closer, I could see "Ground Zero" spray-painted in a 3-D pattern.

I didn't want to be there, so as I was walking I repeated to myself, "Twelve weeks. I can do anything twelve times." I took a deep breath and pushed open the door.

The gym had a cool name. But it was just a gym. It still smelled bad. All the kids wore funny clothes. And it needed better vending machines.

Little kids were blocking the entrance as they took off their shoes. Girls were spinning and giggling on the gymnastics bars. Coaches barked out instructions somewhere far away. Moms and dads socialized nearby. Everyone turned to look at me. So I just stepped around the kids and walked to a chair against the wall. A sign told me to take off my shoes. I sat down.

Past the front desk were three different spaces. The area on the right was full of gymnastics stuff. In the middle was a wide-open floor. On the left, there were steel bars and wooden blocks. It looked like someone stopped in the middle of building a mini-city. It reminded me of an abandoned town in a zombie movie.

Constable Jack appeared from around a corner. He waved to me as he talked to someone at the front desk. He was dressed like a gym coach. He looked a little smaller out of his uniform, but he was still scary. I almost expected him to shout, "Hey, stop! Police!"

"Tricky, come with me," he said instead. He was smiling.

I could feel the workers behind the counter look at me. It felt like everyone was looking at me.

"How are you?" he asked.

"Good, sir." I didn't know what else to say.

"Hah! Call me Coach, or Coach Jack. The class starts in half an hour. But I wanted to give you some lessons first. Most kids in your class have been doing this for a while."

He took off his socks and walked to the parkour section.

"First, this is a gym. We have rules. Be respectful to everyone. Wear the right clothes. Treat the equipment with respect. If something is broken or dirty, clean it or fix it — or tell the staff. Now, take off your socks."

I wondered how many people's bare feet had been on this floor. Gross.

"Let's talk more about parkour," he went on. "It's about running, jumping, climbing and crawling. It's about balance. But it's also about expressing yourself and enjoying movement."

He was quiet for a second, looking at me. I guess he was letting me think about it. It still sounded weird. But I wanted to get this over with.

"Okay," I said.

The lines on Coach's forehead wrinkled. I was glad when he kept talking. I knew I'd get it in time. Hopefully.

"The first thing we're going to learn is the parkour roll. This is important because it helps you keep your momentum when you're running. It also protects you if you fall."

He crouched down on his knees and placed his left hand on the mat. He extended his left leg behind him. Then, he ducked his head under his armpit and kicked his leg over his head. It was the most complicated somersault I'd ever seen.

"The most important thing is to move your head to the side. Tuck your chin into your chest. You roll on your back muscles, not your spine."

I put my left hand on the mat, stretched my left leg behind me and rolled. Just like in grade three Gym class.

"No, that's not it," Coach Jack said. "You rolled along your spine. Parkour is often running outside on hard surfaces. You don't want to roll your spine over rocks."

I tried again. This time, I put both hands on the mat. My fingers and thumbs formed a diamond shape on my left side. I tucked my chin to the side and rolled. This time, nothing but my back muscles touched the floor. I bounced up again.

"Yes, better," Coach said. "Now do it nine more times."

We rolled around on the floor. I tried it on my left and right sides. Other than making me dizzy, it was kind of fun.

That's it? I thought. *This is going to be easy.*

Then we jogged over to the gymnastics area. He pointed me to a balance beam. We walked along it a few times.

"Balance comes from the heel through the arch and out the second toe," he told me.

I was amazed at how well that worked. After that we jogged back to the mini-city. He led me to a box shaped a little like a triangle, wider at the bottom. I'd seen them at my school. But this one was lower. Coach ran at it, placed a hand on top and swung his legs over the side.

"These boxes are called vaults. When we jump over them, it's also called a vault. That's an easy vault to start. But there're plenty of other ways to get over it. This one's called a lazy vault. Then we will try the thief vault."

I looked up at him with wide eyes. I could feel my cheeks turning red. It made me think of how I got here.

"Are you going to tell people about me?" I asked.

"No, of course not," he said. "Maybe we'll just use the lazy vault. Here, you try it."

It didn't look like much. He had just jumped over it. I tried it. I have to admit it made me nervous to run at it. I had too much time to think about what might go wrong.

Coach Jack saw me having trouble. He broke down the movements into small sections. Then it felt a lot easier.

So Coach Jack took me to another, higher box. He took a long run as I watched from beside the vault. He jumped. *Wham*! Both of Coach's hands hit the vault like he was hitting a punching bag. He swung both legs underneath him as he flew through the air. He was over the vault before I knew what had happened. It looked amazing.

He jogged back to me. "That's a Kong vault," he said. "Because you look like a monkey — or King Kong — when you do it. We will work up to that one. But I wanted you to see what you will be able to do."

We kept running through smaller movements: climbing, crawling and swinging on bars.

Then *they* walked into the place. The girl's dark hair was spiky and she was wearing hospital scrubs. I knew they were scrubs because my mom had about a hundred pairs for work.

She had a bunch of metal bracelets on one arm. Her ears were pierced a bunch of times. Her T-shirt said "Sub-Pop." She was amazing. There was a guy with her. He looked a little like a doll or a mannequin. He had perfect hair, expensive running shoes and matching gym clothes. Not that I was all that interested in looking at *him*.

"Hey, Coach," she said. "Can we have some free time?"

"Yeah, but warm-up first, and meet Patrick. Patrick, this is Parker and Jayden. They'll be in your class. Guys, you can call him Tricky."

Was he Parker, or was she?

"I'm Parker, nice to meet you," the girl said. "Yeah, I know. Parker and parkour. But that's not why I'm here. It's just a big, hilarious coincidence. I've heard all the jokes. They're not funny."

"Hey," I said. I wanted to say something about her name. I wanted to promise not to make any jokes. But then he spoke.

"You done this before, Tricky?" Jayden asked. He said "Tricky" like it was painful for him.

"No."

"Didn't think so."

He walked away and did this spinning kick thing. It looked cool. But why was he was doing it before class?

This guy is going to be trouble, I thought.

4 DROPPING IN

From on top of a vault, I looked left and right. I was looking for Parker. I could see small groups of girls in the gymnastics area dancing and singing. They were all in pink, yellow or neon green and had their hair pulled back tight. The smallest kids crowded the open floor. They ran around in circles, with their parents chasing after them. They reminded me of the little kids at Teen Club back home.

Parker wasn't anywhere in the crowd, though. I decided it was the time to practise something new.

Every weekday for the last two weeks had been the same for me. New school. New teachers. Sitting through boring classes. Trying to make friends. At least at parkour, I could talk to Parker. And I could get moving again.

We had been working on our rolls, landings and vaults. We did exercises to get strong. I had even started coming two more times a week for open gyms. Parkour was not the worst thing in the world. But

I didn't feel like admitting it to my mom or Coach.

I had been feeling pretty confident before class. And I was tired of watching Jayden show off. So I was going to jump off the vault into a parkour roll.

All I had to remember was to land on the balls of my feet — that spot behind my toes. And I had to bend my knees just enough and keep my back and feet in the "ready" position.

"You don't want to land with your knees straight," Coach Jack had said. "That will hurt your back. You don't want to bend them too much, either. You gotta be somewhere in the middle."

I felt really good about my rolls. By now I could get over onto my back muscles every time.

I was sure rolling after jumping from a vault would be easy. I had seen Parker practising the move, and I wanted to try it. But I didn't want her to see me try it the first time.

And I didn't want Jayden to see me try it, either. Jayden would be beside her. He never left her alone. Every time I saw Parker, Jayden was trailing behind her like a lost puppy. I'm sure sometimes she didn't even know he was there. I noticed she looked at him like she wasn't really seeing him.

Thinking about the two of them made me nervous. I had to practise before the gym filled up too much. So I jumped off the vault.

It was a bad idea, I know that now. I jumped

too straight. My knees locked. I bounced too high and couldn't get my head out of the way for my roll. My shoulder dug into the mat. That had never happened before.

Nobody needed to yell at me for trying it too soon. The pain in my wrists, neck and back yelled enough. My right cheek even had a bit of burn on it from the mat.

I wanted to sit there and not be noticed. But I didn't get the chance.

"That was awesome, Tricky," a laughing Jayden said.

I turned my head and there they were, right behind me. There's no way they didn't see me. Somehow I had missed them coming into the gym.

I stood quickly. At least Parker was cool. She looked concerned. But then her expression changed to disgust as Jayden kept taunting me.

Coach's voice cut through Jayden's. "Let's take three laps then try the 'bear walks' twice to warm up." He was headed straight for us.

Jayden raised his hand. "Coach, I really want to work on my rolls off the vault. I think Tricky is ready too."

Jayden was smirking. I felt like pushing him off the vault myself.

"Okay, sure," Coach said. He was clearly a little confused. "But after the warm-ups."

After our laps, we lined up behind the vault. I stood at the back.

Jayden was first. He stepped onto the vault and steadied himself. Then he jumped off into his roll.

"Yeah!" Coach said. "What we need to remember is this: don't just step off the vault. You have to jump. Get some distance and lean forward a little. That way, your body is already ready to roll."

I watched student after student try it. Some were better than others. Some asked for an extra mat to cushion their fall. Parker's was nearly perfect. She jumped far ahead, landed with her knees bent just right and then rolled. All in one quick motion.

The vault was the smallest one we had at the gym. It was barely off the ground. But when I stepped on it, I could feel my back and neck tighten.

"Just like you practised it," Jayden yelled from somewhere.

In my mind I could see the stupid grin on his face. I gritted my teeth and stepped off the vault. Again, I landed straight. I wasn't going forward at all. I rolled after that. But landing and rolling felt like two parts instead of one. Coach met me as I went to the back of the line.

"Go forward, not down," he said. "Lean into the roll. And get your hands up so you're ready for the roll."

I watched everyone else go through the line again. It seemed so simple as I watched everyone else leap

forward and roll. This time, when it was my turn, I felt
like I could do it. I stepped up on the vault and jumped
forward quickly. I didn't want to give myself time to
think about what could go wrong.

I reached out ahead of me, but my feet felt
awkward on the landing. I bounced up from landing,
too high again. But this time I tried hard to save the
move. I dove into my roll. The pain in my shoulder
and neck returned.

My hands must have been too low, at my sides.

"Yeah, you almost had it!"

It was Jayden the jerk again. This time everyone else
laughed along with him. I stood up and walked back
toward the line. I wondered why I was even trying.
For two weeks everything had come so easily. Now it
was getting much tougher.

5 PAINFUL REMINDER

I wasn't even back in line before Jayden was hovering. He was like a wasp ready to strike. I could feel him lurking. He'd come into my view, then slip out of sight again.

I didn't need reminders of how badly I had bailed off the vault. But Jayden was reminding everyone. Coach met me at the back of the line again.

"Better. But jump forward more," he said. Then he turned to the group. "Okay, everyone. Take a break."

The class shifted to grab their phones or get water. Jayden grabbed his bottle. He drank it like it was champagne and he had just won a big race.

"Hey, Tricky, I should get your number," he shouted as he clicked on his phone. "We should train together."

All of Jayden's buddies were laughing. They knew I didn't have a phone.

I needed to get away or I would swat him. So I wandered to the water fountains. I had to wait behind little kids who were more interested in pushing the button than in drinking. They'd hit the button and water would shoot up high. Then they'd let go of the button and the water would stop. Their mouths would hang open, dry. And they couldn't figure out what had happened. Finally, I just reached over and held the button for them.

"Can you lift me?" a little girl asked.

I picked her up with one hand and pressed the button with the other. She stuck her mouth into the water so far I thought she might drown.

"That's enough," I said. "Who's next?"

"I am."

It was Parker. I stepped out of the way. I could feel my face getting red.

"Wait, aren't you going to push the button for me?" she asked.

I laughed. But just a little. "You're a big girl."

She smiled. But I felt like a moron. I didn't know what to say.

"Do you have little sisters, Tricky?"

"Nah," I said. "We had Teen Club back home. I'd go there early and play floor hockey with the little kids' group that met ahead of the club."

Parker smiled again. This time she showed off more teeth. "That's so awesome. Were you like a camp counsellor?"

"They asked me to be one. But I didn't have the time."

Well, that was almost true. I had tried it a couple of times. But I didn't want to always have to be there. I hadn't even been paid once before I just stopped going. I felt bad about it after. It had been kind of fun to play with the kids.

Parker bent to take a drink. She even made drinking from a water fountain look cool.

"Your second roll was good," she said. "You'll get the hang of it."

"Thanks, I guess."

"You don't say much, do you?"

"I dunno."

She took another drink. She wiped away water running down her chin. "I think you're a natural," she said, looking at me. "When you have too much time to think about your moves, you hesitate. Maybe you just need to go for it. I think you're more a traceur than a freerunner."

I had no idea what that meant. "A what?"

"Oh, sorry. A traceur does parkour and doesn't worry about fancy kicks. You know, like Jayden does," she said. "Jayden probably does freerunning, not parkour."

"There're two things?"

"Freerunning has more moves — almost like dancing. Parkour is more, I don't know, 'serious,' maybe. Traceurs want to get from here to there in the fastest way possible. Freerunning is more artistic. You can go back over something two or three times just for fun. But that's just my definition. Some people say there's no difference."

I still wasn't sure I understood. It must have shown in my face.

"Well, we better get back," Parker said. "Jayden was telling everyone you're lucky to be alive."

Why couldn't Jayden shut up about my lousy rolls? My face was still red, but now it was from anger.

"Hey, Parker," Jayden shouted to us as we approached. "Have you tried this one?"

He ran at the wall and planted his left foot against it, about a metre high. He jumped and latched onto a vault, pulling himself onto it. It was like he had springs for arms. He dove off it and landed a perfect roll in our direction.

Then he stood up right in front of us.

"We should try that next time at the Bank," he said. "Those statues are perfect for it. Hey, Tricky, how's your neck?" He said my name with a sneer.

"It's good."

We were nose to nose. I wanted to push him out of my face. But I knew Coach Jack was watching. I couldn't figure out why Jayden wanted to bug me so much. It felt like a set-up. He seemed to have it all ready for when people were watching him, especially Parker. I'm not sure why I cared, but I did. It bothered me so much. I had to figure out some way to get back my pride.

Painful Reminder

Coach called us to the mini-city. We gathered around him. Our class was shoulder to shoulder, and Coach patrolled us like we were an army unit ready for a mission.

Without saying anything, he turned and ran at a wall. He planted his foot and lunged high for the ledge. It was three metres up, but he grabbed it with both hands. In one motion, he pulled himself onto it like he was pulling himself out of a swimming pool.

His arm muscles rippled. He was fluid and fast.

"It's a wall climb. It looks impressive to your friends," Coach said from up high. "But it's not hard if you have the upper body strength and technique." He sat down and let himself slide down the wall. "But three metres is too high for you. We'll start here."

The wall in front of us was shorter. It was a little higher than I could stretch and touch with the tips of my fingers. It looked easy enough.

Jayden was first, of course. He sprinted, planted his foot and leaped for the ledge. He whiffed. Instead of springing up, he pushed himself backward and landed back on the floor.

Everyone laughed. Jayden threw his hands up and made a joke.

Parker was next. She wasn't running as fast. She planted her foot and jumped high. She grabbed the ledge, but she didn't have a good grip. She had to slide back down.

A few other kids tried after that. They either didn't get high enough or didn't have enough strength to pull themselves on top.

I didn't know what to expect on my first try. But I remembered what Parker had told me: "Don't think too much."

When everyone cleared a path for my turn, I didn't wait. I just bolted for the wall, planted my foot and jumped. I grabbed the ledge and felt my fingers burn under my weight. I wasn't about to let go, though. I was stuck for half a second. But then I used my feet to keep kicking.

Struggling under my weight, I finally pulled myself up and onto the block. I was the only one to make it on my first try. I stood up. I turned and looked down at the class. I felt like king of the castle. And Jayden was a rascal who could only look up at me.

6 DROPPING OUT

Everyone was cheering. Cheering me. I took two steps toward the end of the block. There was a huge foam mat underneath. I leaped into the air, did a flip, and landed in the foam. For just a second, it felt like I was flying.

Everyone was bouncing in excitement after that. Someone had made it! One by one, they took turns sprinting for the wall. They looked like fighter jets taking off from a runway. One by one, they zoomed at the wall and grabbed at the top ledge.

I looked up and spotted Parker. She was watching from the other side of the lineup. We made eye contact. I thought I was going to burst when she smiled at me.

She came walking over. "What's the secret?" she asked.

My hands were on my knees. My chest was still heaving and it was hard to breath. It took me a second to say anything.

"Go fast," I said. "Don't just jog. You need a strong leg to shoot you high. But don't overthink it."

She smiled and put a hand on my shoulder. I felt a buzz go through my body.

"See?" she said. "I knew you were a natural."

She bumped back into the line. I stepped to the side to get a better view of her second try. This time she was a little bouncier, like everyone else. She started her run, planted her foot, and jumped for the top of the barrier. She caught it with her right hand. She just hung there for a couple of seconds. Then the muscles in her shoulder and back flexed enough for everyone to see.

"Whoa!" someone said.

It's exactly what I was thinking.

Finally, her second hand darted up. I could see she had a better hold. We all started cheering as she slowly pulled up and onto the wall. She scrambled to her feet and did a somersault back onto the mat.

I was there to give her a high-five as she came past me in line. But instead of just slapping her hand, I grabbed it.

"Where did you get those muscles?" I asked her.

"I was in gymnastics for ten years," she said. "Oh, and I was bitten by a radioactive spider."

"Then what took you so long to get up there?"

She let out a big laugh.

I was up next. Feeling light as a balloon, I cleared

the wall just fine. I felt like I could have jumped as high as Coach. The cheering class behind me pushed me to the top.

The shouting kept going for everyone. We all reached the top at least once. I even cheered for Jayden. Then there were flips onto the mat as a reward.

It reminded me of home. Every summer, we'd swim to a small island in the lake and jump from a cliff not much higher than the wall. We'd start by just jumping into the water. Then it became a contest to see who could flip or make the biggest splash. We'd spend all afternoon swimming and jumping. Then we'd just lie on the beach in the sun. That was one of the last times I felt like I belonged. At least, before joining parkour.

By the third try, though, my arms were starting to shake. My muscles felt tight. The skin on my hands was red and rough. I could see my fingers trembling.

"Last time. And then class is over," Coach yelled.

Knowing I'd have to wait a day or two to try the move again, I gritted my teeth. One more climb. My heart pounded a little harder. It was my own personal loudspeaker urging me up the wall.

My jump was good. I grabbed on to the ledge, but my arms weren't ready. I had to hang there for a couple of seconds, shaking, before I found strength to get myself higher. I had to roll on my belly to get onto the platform. Everyone else had the same problem. We looked more like chubby seals flopping around than dolphins leaping from the water.

The edge was starting to get slick with everyone's sweat. *Gross*, I thought as I did my final tumble into the mat below.

That's all I was thinking when Jayden started his final sprint. He was in good shape, so he reached the top of the wall easier than most of us. But as he went for his flip off the wall, he slipped.

His right leg spilled off the edge. His left leg bent at a bad angle, caught on the top of the wall. To make it worse, his momentum carried him sideways, and he fell onto the floor instead of the mat.

Everyone went running, he was yelling so loudly. I kind of felt bad. But the floors were so soft I don't think anyone could have really hurt themselves.

Coach put two hands on Jayden's knee and gently squeezed, looking for damage. Jayden swung his arms at the crowd around him.

"I'm fine!" Jayden said. He stood and took a couple of steps. He looked down at his knee. And then he came running at me.

"You're a sweaty freak," he yelled. "You should've cleaned up after yourself. Why don't you carry a towel?"

I felt his hands on my chest. I banged into someone behind me. I knocked the back of my head into someone's teeth, or forehead, or something.

It probably hurt more than Jayden's fall.

I didn't have time to think about what happened next. I went right back at him. With three or four good steps behind me, I flew at him and pushed him back. He collapsed into the wall, hitting with a thud. For the second time in a couple of minutes, Jayden was yelling on the ground. He didn't get up as quickly this time.

I knew exactly what I had to do. I turned for the door, found my jacket and shoes and left. I heard Coach yelling something at me. But I didn't stick around to answer him. Jayden didn't want me there. I wasn't about to argue anymore.

I didn't need this mess, anyway.

7 SECOND STRIKE

My key turned in the door and I pushed it open. I hadn't headed straight home after school for a while. It was nice not having to worry about going to parkour. Slumped in the recliner in the living room, I grabbed the remote control and clicked on the TV.

My stomach started grumbling right away. I slammed the footrest back down and headed for the kitchen. The two bedrooms, one bathroom, and living room in our apartment were all connected.

I swung the kitchen cupboard doors open and scanned the shelves. I finally found some tortilla chips and an unopened jar of salsa. I cracked a can of cola. It was warm.

My mom kept snacks like that in the cupboard for special occasions. But this was special to me. I was officially dropping parkour. Any second, I expected a knock at the door and Constable Jack to be standing there. He would haul me in front of a judge and that would be it. No more pop or junk food for a long time.

Second Strike

The salsa spilled into a bowl with a satisfying plop. The cola fizzed as it filled an extra-large glass crammed with all twelve ice cubes from a tray in the freezer.

This was better than rushing around after school. And I was always starving at parkour. I slumped back into the chair and found a movie channel. The speakers crackled with heroic-sounding music from some ancient time.

There were sword fights and races across a desert. The hero sneaked into a palace to steal a jewelled dagger from under the pillow of an evil king. He was just about to get away when a bird landed on the windowsill and let out a shriek. The evil king woke up and sounded an alarm.

Clang, clang, clang! He beat on a gong.

Guards burst in through every door. They appeared from behind every curtain. The hero ran. First, he did two speed vaults and a wall climb. Then he latched onto a flag pole and climbed it. And finally, he performed a perfect dive roll through a window into a room filled with beautiful women.

It was all parkour. All the stunts in the movie were parkour moves.

"Oh, come on!" I shouted. "Is somebody trying to tell me something?"

The movie wasn't very good. But I couldn't stop watching. It was amazing to watch the actors (and their stunt doubles) do so much with parkour.

Freerunner

They balanced on ledges and hung from ropes. They jumped from rooftop to rooftop, rolling and gliding to safety.

My legs were twitching. My chips and salsa were gone. I tried eating a bowl of cereal. After the cereal and the movie were done, I went to the kitchen to dump the bowl in the dishwasher. There, on the fridge, was my letter from Coach Jack. I read again how I was expected to do parkour for twelve weeks.

My signature was at the bottom.

I turned off the TV, threw the remote onto the couch and grabbed my shoes. I zipped up my jacket in the elevator. When the doors opened on the ground floor, I glanced to my left and saw the bus coming from a block away.

There was a courtyard with plants and playground equipment in the middle of our apartment complex. Instead of heading around it, I went straight through it. I grabbed the monkey bars and swung through them. I did a speed vault over a park bench. I ran along the edge of a cement planter, jumped off and did a parkour roll along the grass.

It was the first time I'd used my moves outside the gym. It got me to the bus stop with time to spare. I couldn't wait to tell Parker. But only after telling Coach I was sorry and asking for a second chance.

★ ★ ★

Coach Jack was in his office. He was writing in a notebook.

He waved me inside without looking up from his work. The door closed behind me with a soft click. I stood, waiting for instructions.

There was no ticking clock to tell me how long I was standing there. I had no phone to tell me what time it was, either. It didn't seem like Coach was going to tell me to sit down. Was he giving me the silent treatment?

The scratching of his pen was loud in the silence. All I wanted was for him to start chewing me out for what had happened the night before. He was almost always smiling and happy, but I expected him to at least yell at me. The silence was worse.

"Sorry," he said, finally.

I shifted from side to side. I waited for the fallout.

"You missed class," he said.

"Yeah."

"Are you going to stay for drop-in tonight?"

Now, I really didn't know what to say. I had been expecting him to kick me out of class and tell me to report for fingerprinting.

"Uh, yeah. If I'm allowed."

"I don't really like baseball. But let's call this strike two. You know what that means, right?"

I didn't think he really wanted me to answer, so I just nodded.

"I only have a couple of things to say," Coach added. "First, you need to apologize for pushing Jayden and ask him if he's okay. Second, he accused you of leaving unsafe equipment behind you. That's not good, if it's true."

"But —" I tried to interrupt.

"That's all I'm going to say. Jayden is here. You two talk. Then report back to me after class."

My head hanging low, I turned and walked out of the office. I suppose I should have said "thanks." He didn't punish me (at least not yet).

I shut the door behind me as quietly as I had opened it. I could see Jayden and his friends practising their vaults. As I walked over to them, I rehearsed in my head what I was going to say.

"Hope you brought your towel," Jayden said.

"Whatever," I said. "It was wet when I got there. It wasn't me."

"Then you have to clean it up. Everyone here knows that."

"Fine, I'm sorry I didn't clean it up. Coach wants to see us after."

"Yeah, I know. He told me. I'm sorry for accusing you and calling you a 'freak.'"

We just stood there for a second. I don't think he believed I was sorry. I know I didn't believe him.

8 THIRD STRIKE

Parker arrived late for the drop-in session. When she got there, she and I said hello to each other. But that was about all I said to her that night. She mostly sat on a stack of mats, laughing and talking with the gymnastics girls. I was pretty sure she was mad at me for pushing Jayden and storming out of the building.

A constant stream of people came and went in front of Parker. She looked like a queen greeting her royal subjects. Boys and girls would bounce up to her as they took water breaks. They'd pop up onto the mats. She'd hug them and they'd laugh. Then they'd scurry off back to class with big grins on their faces. No, she wasn't a queen, she was a rock star.

I kept watching her all class. I was sure Jayden was watching her too. But I doubt she looked at either of us. It made me like her even more. It seemed she had other, more important things to worry about. I wanted to know what those things were. Plus, she was really cute.

Eventually, I just gave up thinking about Parker and worried about parkour. A row of three vaults sat in front of me. Sweat dripped into my eyes. My T-shirt was soaked through. I had my hands on my knees most of the time, searching for a way to get more air into my lungs.

Vaults were as much fun as climbing walls. We had focused on them even more than walls in our classes.

"A good vault is as good as gold," Coach had said. "If you crack a good vault, you get the gold."

Coach wandered past a few times, answering questions and offering advice. He would walk up and down the lines as if he was inspecting his troops. Then he'd duck into his office and stuff his head back into more paperwork.

I glanced up at the clock. There were only about fifteen minutes left in the drop-in session. The place was nearly empty. A few of the older teens in advanced parkour classes wandered around. They were in charge. But they weren't paying much attention to anyone else. This was the time to try new moves.

We had strict rules about vaults. We could try lazy vaults or safety vaults by ourselves. If we wanted to practise our dash or Kong vaults, we had to get a coach to act as a spotter. But the coaches weren't around. And everyone else was doing whatever they wanted anyway.

"Kong vaults are simple," I heard Jayden saying. "Most people can't do a dash vault properly."

Third Strike

I let out a huge groan. Jayden was always saying things he couldn't prove. He talked really loudly. And he talked a lot too. I turned my head to avoid listening to him. But it didn't work. Even from across the floor, I couldn't help but hear him.

I was in a spot where I could watch Jayden without being obvious. He was set up across the gym with his two best friends, Brody and Brock. They had two vaults out and were trying dash and Kong back-to-back. They were doing okay, I guess. I was worried about my safety vaults and doing them quickly. Without a coach, I wasn't going to try Kong vaults. Jayden and his friends had been doing parkour for a couple of years. I had being doing this for only a few weeks.

My routine was safety–lazy–shoulder roll over the three boxes. I ran at the first box. I placed my right hand on top of it, followed by my left foot. Then my right leg swung through the middle and I was over to the other side. Then I took two giant steps and placed my left hand on the top of the second box. My right leg drove up over the box to get me to the other side.

The last box I rolled over on my shoulder and back. I did this a bunch of times in a row, just to make sure I was totally confident. Then I walked back to the beginning and reset the boxes. They weren't heavy, and you had to secure them with Velcro straps on the bottom.

"You're looking good," Parker said from behind me. "Pretty soon you'll be teaching those moves."

I grabbed a towel from beside one of the boxes. "Thanks. I'm just trying to get the basics right."

"You can't do the fancy stuff without the simple stuff first," Parker said, nodding.

"You're not doing parkour today?"

"Nah, I needed a break. But my mom drove me here, so I had to come. I was going to stay home, but she wanted me out of the house."

Brock and Brody suddenly ran between us. If we were any closer, they would have knocked us down. Brock did a dash vault and Brody did a Kong vault over my boxes. Then they came running back.

Parker and I stepped aside. They were howling with laughter. I couldn't tell what was supposed to be so funny.

Brock took the first vault without any trouble. Brody ran around the first box and bailed on the second. He tried a dash vault. But he couldn't get his feet over the barrier and landed hard on his back.

Parker and I ran over to him. He was just lying there on the ground.

"You okay, Brody?" Parker asked him.

"Oh, my back," he said. "Did it look awesome? Was anybody recording me? Did you have your phones out?"

We helped him to his feet.

"No, sorry," I said. "I don't have one."

"I don't carry mine when I'm doing parkour," Parker said.

Brody stood suddenly. His head was down, like he was hiding from us. He turned and ran away.

"Anyway," Parker said. "I was just about to leave. I thought I'd say goodbye."

"Sure. I'm just going to do a couple more and then leave too."

"You want a ride home?"

"Nah, I'm only a short bus ride away."

"Okay, see you later."

"See ya."

I moved back to my starting spot. My arms and legs were cooled off. But talking to Parker always gave me lots of extra energy. I was ready to try my Kong vault. I ran full speed and planted both hands on top of the box. Then I slammed hard to the ground.

Something was wrong. I was too confused to know what exactly. All I knew was my vault was somehow messed up and I bailed just like Brody had. I looked around. Parker was running toward me.

"You okay?" she shouted.

Jayden and his buddies were all laughing in a group. They were holding their phones. They had been recording me fall. They had set me up.

I stood up and ran full speed into the centre of them. I started shoving and swinging. I didn't care who I hit. I didn't care about parkour or what would happen to me.

9 LAST CHANCE

Phones went flying when I crashed into Jayden and his buddies. The whole group of us spilled into some mats stacked to the side of the training area. Through the chaos, I kept thinking I was glad Parker hadn't been sitting on the mats. I would have knocked her off backwards. She probably would have hurt herself.

Instead, Parker was yelling at us to stop. I heard her. But I couldn't stop. I grabbed Jayden by the collar of his shirt. I pinned him on his back and pushed his shoulders down against the mat. I was forcing breath from between my clenched teeth. I sounded like a bull running at a bullfighter.

Just as fast, though, Jayden flipped me onto my back. He didn't look like he was much of a fighter. But he was sure able to push me around. I was suddenly worried. I wrenched and writhed under him. I arched my back and managed to get my feet under me. I stood and we faced each other.

On the spongy, soft floors, it was hard to gain any

advantage. We kept each other close. Then I spotted Parker. She wasn't yelling anymore. She looked angry. And sad too. I realized what we must have looked like. I just kind of gave up after that.

Jayden dropped me again. He pulled back his fist. I prepared for a punch to the nose. I was tired of him pushing me around. But I was also tired of fighting him. This wasn't what parkour was about, anyway.

The punch never came. Jayden just held me to the ground. He must have been able to see I wasn't going to fight back.

Besides, I was exhausted. After what was probably only ninety seconds of "fighting," I was done. Coach sprinted up to us and grabbed Jayden. He yanked him to one side. He pulled me off the mat like a ragdoll. Before I knew it, I was standing again.

"Both of you, in my office!"

It was the first time I'd ever seen Coach Jack angry. His eyes were big, black holes under furious, lowered eyebrows.

Everyone stopped shouting. Jayden led the way. I marched behind him. Jayden sat beside the desk. I sat in the chair near the door. Outside, Coach was talking to Brody, the kid who fell. Brody turned on his phone and gave it to Coach. It was obvious they were watching the video.

He shooed Brock and Brody away with a wave of his arm. They scurried to grab their gear and ran for the door. Then it was Parker's turn. Parker didn't talk for very long.

It ended with Coach slapping his forehead with a meaty forehand. I could hear the slap through the glass.

Jayden and I were probably a metre apart. I could have reached out and mussed his perfect hair — which was still perfect, even after rolling around on the mat. Coach let us sit there for ten minutes. When he finally came into his office, he didn't even ask us what happened.

I braced for it. This was my third strike, right? It was time for my exit.

"Listen to me," he said. "In six weeks, our club is going to participate in a parkour demonstration. You will both be there. We will see your moves. Maybe, if you're good enough, you'll get a free T-shirt or something. Until then, you call a ceasefire."

I glanced at Jayden. He looked up at the same time and smirked. It made me angry again. I needed more than ever to show him he couldn't intimidate me.

"You guys seem to need a measuring stick to see who is better at this stuff," Coach continued. "Maybe the demo day will show you who is boss. Then you can stop the fighting."

Coach reached into his desk drawer and pulled out a stack of colourful brochures. He peeled two of them from under a rubber band and handed us one each.

"Read this," he said. "Write the date in your calendar. I expect you to be prepared. Maybe, just maybe, it will also teach you what you're doing here. You're missing the point of parkour. It's not about seeing who is best. It's about testing yourselves and overcoming barriers. I'm hoping you will figure that out for yourselves."

I grabbed the brochure. But I didn't look at it. I was still angry. As far as I was concerned, I might not make another six weeks of this.

"Okay, Patrick, go home," Coach said.

I looked up, stunned. Jayden had a wide-eyed look too. The smirk was gone. Coach waved me out of the office. I jumped to my feet, and bolted through the door. I didn't bother looking behind me. I turned a corner and nearly ran into Parker.

"Tricky," she said. "What happened?"

"Nothing, really," I said. "But Jayden's still in there."

"I told Coach what I saw. That Jayden and his buddies were up to something. That they knew you were going to fall and were ready to film it. That I saw you run into them. I said you stuck up for yourself, but didn't throw a punch."

That left me speechless, which was rare for me. "Thanks."

I really wanted to hug her. I wanted to run out the door with her before Jayden left Coach's office. Instead, she reached for my hand. I started to get really nervous, and then she grabbed the brochure. I had forgotten that I was still holding it.

"This looks amazing!"

I hadn't even read it yet. She handed it back to me and I unfolded it. I scanned it quickly. I saw the date for the Healthy Habits Day event. It was the day that ended the twelve weeks I had promised Coach Jack. I read the part about "hundreds of kids and parents in attendance." The thought of performing in front of a crowd made me queasy.

"You need to come with me this weekend to the Bank," Parker said. "It's this totally cool park we've found to train. You have to start practising outside. It's totally different outside."

Jayden appeared just as Parker was talking. I saw his head snap up when she mentioned practising together.

"Yeah, for sure, thanks. I'd love to go with you." I admit it, I said that loud enough that Jayden heard me.

We watched Jayden sneak past us to his shoes and jacket. Parker placed her hand on my forearm. We looked each other in the eye for a few seconds. It might have been the best few seconds of my life.

Then she looked at Jayden.

"We'll talk more on Friday, okay, Tricky? My mom is here. I gotta go."

"Sure."

She followed Jayden as he pushed open the front door. "Jayden, wait . . ."

I didn't care if they left together. Even though I knew she was going to make sure he wasn't kicked out of class. Really, it didn't matter to me anymore. I could finally stop worrying about what Jayden was going to do to me, now that I had a girl like Parker on my side.

10 CATCH ME IF YOU DARE

The girl didn't look like Parker. I'd arrived where we'd planned to meet. I spotted someone doing what looked like a backward cartwheel. Her back was to me. She suddenly jumped back and flipped head over heels. Just like that, she was standing on her feet again. It was Parker.

"That was cool," I said.

"Thanks," Parker said. "We used to do them all the time in gymnastics. I wasn't sure I could still do one."

"A cartwheel?"

"It's called a back handspring. I could teach you."

"Maybe some other time," I said.

She laughed and touched my arm. We walked together into the park. A cloudless sky meant the sun reflected into our eyes. I didn't need my jacket, so I unzipped it and left it on the ground.

My arms felt a little cool. But I knew in just a few minutes I'd be warm enough.

"What are back handsprings for?"

"My floor routine," she said. "You know the one where girls run from one corner of the mat to the other, jumping and spinning? You've probably watched it on the Olympics."

"Oh, that one."

We didn't have a TV when I was younger. But I didn't want to tell her that. And I don't remember ever wanting to watch the Olympics when we did get a TV. The Games always seemed kind of silly to me.

"You still do gymnastics?" I asked.

"I gave it up last year. It made my mom really mad."

"That's why you're doing parkour?"

"Totally. Everyone is so chilled out. We try and help each other. In gymnastics, it seemed like some girl was always angry or crying. I had been surrounded by basically the same girls since I was four. I needed a break from all the drama."

I felt kind of bad when she said that. She saw lots of drama when Jayden and I started pushing each other around.

She must have been thinking the same thing. "Well, I thought parkour was chill," she said. "Then you arrived, and all of a sudden people are getting all aggro."

I could feel my cheeks getting red. It wasn't my fault, I wanted to say. Jayden was the guy who flipped out for no reason. Sure, I pushed him around. But he was the one who took a swing at me.

We sat there for a couple of minutes without saying anything. I could see why Parker called this park the Bank. There was a statue for each of the provinces. The taller ones kind of looked like bank machines. The park wasn't very big, with a path through some flowers and a couple of sculptures. A fountain sat in the centre. A low stone wall circled the whole thing.

"I didn't want any trouble," I said, finally. "I guess I just kind of snapped."

"Jayden can be kind of a jerk sometimes. But he's always been nice to me. We started parkour at the same time. You know, he used to be in martial arts. Actually, I think he could've done a lot worse. I'm glad it didn't go any further."

Her words felt like a punch to the stomach. The old Tricky from Red Rock would have probably left right then. If she was such good friends with Jayden, why was she here with me?

I decided Red Rock was a long time ago.

"Let's stop talking about it," I said. "We're here to, what did you call it again? Trace?"

"Yeah. Do you know what it means? I wasn't sure the other day."

"Not really, I guess. Do you? Like, for real?"

"You'll have to catch me to find out!"

With that, Parker was off and running along the edge of the stone wall. She jumped to the grass and rolled. I followed as quickly as I could.

It felt different, just like when I got through the playground at my building. At the gym, I'd land on a soft mat if I fell. Outside it was dirt and rocks. The wall was only about a metre off the ground. I jumped between some shrubs, rolled and sprang up on my feet.

Parker was far ahead of me. But I could see her path. I turned right and took three big strides toward a handrail for a speed vault. I planted my left foot and kicked my right foot high in the air. I grabbed the rail with my left hand.

I chased her up some stairs. The park opened into a central courtyard. In the centre, the ten stone statues formed a half-circle.

We vaulted over the first one. We jumped onto the second and climbed on top of it. Then we did some precision jumps from statue to statue. I crouched down to build tension in my legs. I stretched out my arms above my head and forward. I jumped and brought my knees up into my chest. I went from Saskatchewan to Manitoba to Ontario. Quebec and Ontario were the tallest. When Parker landed on Quebec, she placed her hands along the edge and let her legs drop over the side. She jumped off, landed on the balls of her feet, and kept running. She hardly made any sound at all.

I decided to also skip the smaller Maritime statues. But instead of jumping across to Quebec, I wanted to try something different.

I put my hands on the ledge of Ontario. Quebec was less than two metres away. I jumped for it, letting my feet contact the rough stone first. I grabbed the top of the statue and let myself fall to the ground. It wasn't far and I was able to hit the ground running.

When I caught up to Parker she was sitting on the edge of the fountain. It was dry, though, and I could already see it would be our next obstacle.

We continued like that for another thirty minutes. We would run from one part of the park to another, trying our moves and coming up with new ways to get around the obstacles.

It was the best day I'd had since moving to the city.

"That was awesome, thanks," I said. We'd finally stopped and were sitting on B.C.

"You're welcome," she said. "Jayden and I come here all the time. It's great practice."

And, just like that, there was his name again. I wasn't sure if I'd ever get rid of that guy.

11 TRAINING DAYS

A weird energy greeted me my first day back at the gym. It felt like I was in a bubble. But I could see and hear everyone talking at the same time. Healthy Habits Day and the parkour demo were only six weeks away. It was all I could think about and all anyone seemed to care about.

"What path are you going to take?"

"I wonder if they'll have eight-foot walls."

"I bet they will have ten-footers."

"I heard Jake Diamond from Montreal is coming. He's the king."

I didn't know what any of it meant. I really didn't care, either. I just wanted to hang out with Parker and have some fun at the gym. During the warm-up, Jayden was walking around with a silly grin on his face. He always started class with his martial arts routine. He would jump into the air and spin. He would punch the air and throw kicks.

Thankfully, Coach gathered us for the warm-up

drills so I didn't have to watch much more of that. The drills were always hard work. We had to work on our upper-body strength and our core muscles. That meant a lot of exercises that kind of looked like push-ups, sit-ups and pull-ups. But they were always just a bit different and a bit harder.

"You'll never get anywhere without training and working," Coach yelled. "You need to be strong to do parkour. We have six weeks before the demo. So get ready. It's about to get a lot harder from here."

Coach was the strongest person I'd ever met. His muscles had muscles. I wasn't sure I wanted to know what his "harder" workouts would be like.

I found out anyway. After a couple of laps of running, we moved to the vaults. There were four vaults, with three of us stationed at each. All we had to do was walk up to the vault, put our hands on top of it and pull ourselves onto it. It would have been simple just once. Even doing it five times was manageable. But doing two sets of ten dips was harsh. We had to "snap to the top" and slowly lower ourselves back down again.

"Keep your elbows in and your chest over the top of the vault," Coach instructed. "If you are having trouble, use your toes to help you get up."

I was having trouble. After the dips, my arms felt like jelly. A two-minute break was not enough for them to feel any better. I grabbed a drink at the fountain and jogged back to where Coach was standing.

"Drop and give me ten!"

Great, push-ups. At least I was getting used to them by now. Normally, I could do ten push-ups without much worry. But this was not a normal workout.

I glanced around at the other kids. Everyone was huffing and puffing. Parker's face was beet red. Jayden was sweating so much his perfect hair was starting to look less perfect.

"For your next ten, put your hands together." Coach was kidding, right?

Everyone groaned. We were all struggling now. Most kids had to put their knees on the floor to take some of the weight away. I refused to do that. I was going to finish without cutting any corners.

I spotted Jayden looking at me. By the eighteenth push-up, we were the only two with our knees off the ground.

"This looks too easy for our friends Jayden and Tricky," Coach yelled. "So put your hands wider than your shoulders. Let's see how many we can count to."

Just preparing for my first push-up in the wide position was super hard. I felt like I had no power at all. I could hear everyone struggling. I took a deep breath, let it out, and then pushed up. The chest muscles near my shoulders were on fire. I used every fibre in my body to do one push-up.

As a class, we counted to four. Most kids dropped out, even with their knees on the ground. It was just Jayden and me left by the time we counted six.

I had no idea how I would make it to seven. As I lowered myself to the ground I worried that I would not get back up.

Everyone was up on their feet watching Jayden and me.

"Come on, Tricky," some kids yelled. "Come on, Jayden. You guys can do this!"

"Who is going to get to number seven?" Coach shouted.

I lowered myself, my arms shaking the entire way. I held it there for a second. But I knew the longer I waited, the harder it was going to be to push up again. I closed my eyes and tucked my chin down toward my chest.

With all my strength, I pushed off the ground.

"Yeah! That's it, keep going!"

The class was really cheering us on. I did not want Jayden to "win." I clenched my teeth and then let out a deep breath as my arms straightened.

"Seven!"

Then I collapsed back down. There was no way my body was going to let me do any more. Sweat was dripping into my eyes, but I spotted Jayden in the same position.

"Seven! That was awesome, guys. Great work," Coach said.

I let out a huge breath and looked up at Jayden. He wasn't smirking or smiling anymore.

Did I have his attention, finally? Was he going to stop bugging me? Or did this mean he was going to push me even harder?

I stood and stretched out my arms. We were still looking at each other.

"I guess you're not going anywhere," he said.

It seemed like a silly thing to say. He was not going to scare me off.

"I guess not."

12 NINJA TRICKERY

I had to go to the mall. It wasn't to steal, either. I had never stolen anything before the headphones. And I was never going to again. But being banned from the mall made me see it as the most exciting place in Ottawa. It was the forbidden fortress inside the walled city. It didn't help that Parker and her friends invited me. They were going to shop and then walk around the ByWard Market.

I was stuck. The mall security had banned me for one year. They had my picture in the security office and everything. But hanging out with Parker was too tempting.

I came up with a plan. I told Parker I had to study until five o'clock.

"On a Saturday night?" she asked.

"Yeah, my mom is really strict about that. I do homework every day until five. But then I'm free. I could meet you after."

It wasn't a lie. My mom was strict about homework.

She just wasn't that strict about weekends.

"I'm going to meet Parker and some friends tonight," I told my mom. "Maybe we'll grab a BeaverTail or something. She is shopping for something first."

"She? Ooh! Parker is a girl! You got any money?"

I couldn't help smiling at my mom. She knew my weak spots.

"A few bucks," I answered.

She handed me twenty more and her cell phone. "Be home at a decent hour. Say 'hi' to Parker for me!"

"Thanks, Mom."

I grabbed my shoes and coat and headed out the door before she started making kissy faces. Parker and I had planned to meet at six. But by the time I got there, Parker was nowhere to be found.

I texted her: Hey, it's Tricky. You here?

Parker: Wow! You have a phone. Congratulations!

Me: Mom's phone. I'm at the BeaverTails place.

Parker: Great. We are nearly finished. Meet us at Run 'n' Racket. I'm trying on shoes. You can help me pick.

My guts started churning. I didn't want to sneak into the mall. I was sure I'd get caught and Parker would see it all happen. But I didn't want to stay outside. She might think something was wrong with me.

I reached into my pocket and pulled out my baseball cap. I zipped up my jacket so the collar covered most of my mouth. I caught a glimpse of my reflection. There was no way anyone could recognize me. I kind of looked like a ninja.

Still, I was breaking a promise and I hated myself for it.

Just for a minute. Then we are gone, I thought.

I crossed the market and headed into the mall through the same entrance where Coach first nabbed me. Dozens — probably hundreds — of people were coming and going.

"Okay, I got this," I said to myself.

I had to stop right away. Two security guards stood talking to each other outside a coffee shop. I ducked behind a group of kids with baseball caps walking slowly past them. They were wearing "Confederation HS Basketball" jackets. I was just another player, although definitely the shortest one.

As soon as we had passed the guards, I peeled off from them. I walked down a corridor to my right.

No way! Another security guard. His blue dress shirt with darker blue vest were obvious. And he was coming right at me. For a second, I could have sworn we made eye contact.

Was it extra-security night? I couldn't believe my luck.

But someone walked between us and I turned to look at something in a window. Uh oh. It was a women's store. I had to turn away unless I wanted people to think I was interested in buying a bikini.

Thankfully, something caught the guard's eye. He was staring at hot dogs rolling on a grill. This was my chance to get around him. But I was blocked by some benches. I took a couple of big steps, and then placed both hands and my right foot on the back of the bench. I popped into the air, throwing my left leg between my right foot and hand. I landed quietly on the other side. In the gym, it would have been called a safety vault.

It was so fast, nobody noticed. At least, that's what I hoped. I sneaked a glance as I walked down the other side of the aisle. The security guy was buying a hot dog. But, man, two minutes in the mall and I'd already leaped over a bench dodging security. If I kept this up, I was going to draw too much attention to myself.

My phone buzzed. It was Parker.

We're at the checkout. We'll meet you outside R 'n' R.

That was a relief. I was feeling more hopeful that I could get away with this. I still had to make my way up to the second floor, though. I stepped onto the escalator and started the ride up.

I glanced ahead. Seriously?

Another security guard was about to step onto the down escalator. We would have to pass right by each other. I didn't want to risk it. I took two steps up, placed one hand on either side of the escalator, braced myself and spun over the railing. It was a reverse vault, mostly. Now, I was headed down again with the guard behind me.

I needed another route. I shuffled toward the escalator and started up again. The Run 'n' Racket was in view at the end of the corridor.

My phone buzzed.

Meet you downstairs.

Great. That's just where I had come from. Now I was following Parker. I thought I spotted her, and I hoped she'd look back and join me. That way, I could blend into another crowd. But she never looked back. I was coming down the escalator. Those same two security guards were still at the entrance. If I kept walking, I'd go right past them. I had another idea.

I grabbed the railing and did another reverse vault. Now I was standing on the ledge, about two metres off the ground. But the escalator was shielding me from the guards. I let myself go, landing softly on the balls on my feet. I had more momentum than I'd guessed, though. I had to drop into a parkour roll to absorb some of the fall. I stood and walked calmly toward the door where Parker was waiting.

"Were you just doing parkour in the mall?"

I smiled. My face was red from exercise and embarrassment. She didn't have to wait for my answer. A big smile spread across her face.

"That's just crazy nonsense!" she said. "You are so my hero right now."

Hey, it was just a little ninja trickery. But it really felt amazing to think I had impressed her.

13 ZOMBIE APOCALYPSE

When we got to the entrance, I stepped ahead of Parker and her two friends — Naomi and Shoana — to open the door for them. It was also my escape from mall security. I was finally outside the Rideau Centre again. I unzipped my jacket a little and lifted the ball cap from my eyes.

I took a deep breath of the cooler night air. Parker's invitation to do something fun — and my little disappearing act from security — made me feel good. Maybe I was finally starting to figure out this new city. The shoplifting and my fight with Jayden were a little further behind me.

"Seriously, what made you decide to jump from the escalator there?" Parker asked me.

"I am still trying to figure out when you do this stuff. You know, parkour," I said. "Like, can you get a job doing it?"

They laughed as we crossed the street into the ByWard Market. Shoana jabbed Naomi with her elbow and whispered something in her ear, all the while staring at me. They both giggled.

"You could be a stuntman," Naomi said.

"And you will be able to save your girlfriend from the zombie apocalypse," Shoana said.

Parker rolled her eyes at her friends. "Okay, that's enough," she said. "What you should do, Tricky, is those obstacle course races on TV. You could win a million dollars."

I liked the idea of a million dollars. And being in the movies would be awesome. But zombies only made me think of one thing.

"Well, all of those sound good," I said. "But what sounds better right now is food."

We gorged ourselves on hot dogs and poutine. I dug my fork into the French fries. The cheese was so melty under the bubbling gravy, it felt like I could pull it forever from the box and it would never break. The hot dog came rolled in pastry. I covered mine in mustard and relish.

Parker and I shared a BeaverTail — the long, flat donut was covered with chocolate sauce and peanut butter candies. We ripped it in half. Her hand darted out and scooped up all the candy that fell off the top.

"Mmm, you're too slow," she said as she crunched.

We spent another hour wandering the tents that held the ByWard Market's shops.

Most were filled with rows of bright red tomatoes,

green peppers, potatoes, corn on the cob and every kind of apple you'd ever heard of. One whole tent was devoted to maple syrup: cans and glass bottles in shades of gold and bronze, maple candies and maple cookies. Still others sold buckets of exotic flowers with delicate petals on thick green stems. Those stalls were my favourite. They smelled kind of like the forest back home after a sudden, hard rainstorm.

Parker and her friends pored over handmade jewellery for sale. They held up flowing dresses in pink and green. They tried on sandals.

I zipped into a candy store and came out with five dollars' worth of licorice for my mom. Ottawa suddenly felt like a very different city. It felt smaller. Everyone said hello to us. Maybe I'd been too quick to dismiss Ottawa as a place that did not want me.

Parker and I said goodbye to her friends when Naomi's mom came to pick them up.

"Do you guys want a ride?" Naomi's mom asked us.

"My mom is coming soon," Parker added. "We will give Tricky a ride home."

"Do you want us to wait? It's getting awfully dark out."

"Yeah, you don't want to get trapped by the zombies!" a laughing Naomi said as she climbed into the back seat.

Parker closed the car door on her friend and laughed. "We'll be fine. Thanks for the offer."

The car sped away and we turned to walk back through the market. It was suddenly quiet too. Most of the tents were closed and lights were turning off for the night. We could see shadows working around corners, but we did not see many people.

Parker and I looked at each other. She tried to smile and so did I.

"I can take the bus," I said.

"And leave me here alone? Thanks a lot!" She was laughing as she said it. "It's fine," she added. "We almost drive right past your place on the way home."

Parker was shivering a little. Her head was turning from one direction to the other.

"You okay?" I asked.

"Yeah, totally. But let's get going. This place is starting to weird me out. We have to meet my mom on the other side of the mall."

Something crashed right in front of us. Parker shouted and I jumped. One of the farmers loading her truck had dropped a box of tomatoes. Red goo spread across the pavement.

"Now where?" I said.

Parker took two big strides and jumped for the wall of a building next to us. She burst past the spilled tomatoes and planted her foot on the wall while gripping the ledge to pull herself up.

"Nice!" I said.

I followed, jumping off my right foot and planting

my left on the wall. It was an easy escape, thanks to a wall jump.

"Hey, cool moves!" someone said from a doorway. Two men laughed a creepy laugh. They were hidden in darkness. We scooted past them down the sidewalk.

"Are they following us?" Parker asked.

"Nah," I said. But I wasn't sure.

Just to be safe I waved Parker to follow me to our right. We turned a corner quickly. Some park benches stretched out down the middle of the sidewalk. I led the way this time, going at them quickly.

I placed my hands on the back of a bench and vaulted over it. Parker was right behind me. We were now far away from the two weirdos.

"That was fun," I said.

"We have a few minutes to kill," Parker answered, looking at her phone.

We walked along a low stone fence that looked down on a park below us. I vaulted over some posts cemented into the ground. They were to keep cars off the sidewalk, I guess. Parker ran along their tops, one by one. It looked like she was flying. She barely landed on each before springing to the next one.

I ran ahead. I jumped onto a fancy, old-fashioned street light and spun around it with my hands. We sprinted across the street, vaulting over more of the concrete barriers. We danced along the edge of some flower beds and did a gate vault over a fence.

A statue of an old soldier greeted us at the end of the sidewalk. The path circled around it. We rounded the corner, only to stumble upon three people staring into their cell phones, leaning against a fence.

"Ah!" Parker shouted again, but then started laughing.

The three people didn't even look at us. They just swayed a little in our direction, mumbling something about "brainless kids."

We kept running.

"He said 'brains,'" I said.

Parker was laughing so hard she could barely vault over the fence. We cleared it and did parkour rolls on the grass.

"We are so far from where we need to be," Parker said.

We turned back and found another path back to the street.

"There she is," Parker said.

We crossed to where a black SUV was waiting. It was so sleek and shiny it glowed in the night. Parker's mom saw us and started the engine. It growled to life.

"Mom, step on it. To Tricky's, I mean Patrick's house."

"Were those guys real zombies?" I asked Parker.

"At least now we know we can survive the apocalypse."

Her mom looked at us like we were losing it. But she managed a small smile. "I don't want to know," she said.

I looked around me as we pulled away. The leather seats were cool and smooth. The cabin glowed from a digital screen in the centre. It dawned on me as I pulled on my seatbelt: Parker's family was loaded.

That bit of nagging doubt suddenly crept back into my head. Why was Parker hanging out with a poor kid from the boonies, anyway? Maybe Jayden was right. Maybe he and Parker belonged together. Parker and I didn't have anything in common.

14 BEAST MODE

They looked like boring monkey bars to me. But Coach called them laché bars. They were tucked off in the corner of our gym. I had barely paid them any attention until the moment Coach led us to them at the next practice. There were three steel posts bolted to the floor. I reached out and grabbed one. A dull rattle answered back.

Bars stretched between the wall and posts. Everything was connected by rivets, nuts and bolts. It looked like something you'd see on a construction site.

The first bar was just above my head. I jumped up and grabbed it with both hands.

"Demo day is coming up, and it's time to start the really hard work," Coach said. "These are easy, fun skills to add to your runs. You've all been on monkey bars before, and some of you have tried these. So let's get busy."

He jumped up and grabbed the nearest bar with both hands. He kicked his legs out for momentum, and after three big swings, he was nearly flat on his back in the air. He let go, reached out and grabbed the second bar. He repeated that between the second and third bars. Then the third and fourth. When he reached the end, he threw himself straighter into the air. He twisted in mid-air and grabbed the bar before heading back toward us.

"Just practise swinging on one bar," he said. "Then let go and land properly. Don't try swinging from bar to bar yet. That will come later."

He walked us down to the far post.

"When you swing and land, run for this post and do a twist around it before you head back into line."

I stepped up for my first swing on the bar. When I grabbed it, I felt the skin on my palms pinch. I had to readjust my grip a little. I kicked my legs forward to get as much momentum as possible. It was an easy thing to do. But it was also more painful than I had guessed.

My hands felt chapped almost from the start. But I wanted to get a feel for how much strength I'd need to swing from bar to bar. So I kicked my legs hard.

I let go and reached for the second bar. I was still too far away from it, so I landed on the balls of my feet with bent knees. I ran at the post and twisted around it.

After fifteen minutes, it felt like the skin on my hands was cracking. I was glad when Coach called for a water break. Pushing the button on the water fountain felt strange after so much swinging and twisting.

I was hoping Coach would take it easy on us after that. I was wrong.

"Ready for a workout?" he shouted. "Hands and knees, friends."

Everyone in class groaned. That meant quadrupedal movements. QMs had us crawling on the floor.

"Let's do the monkey," Coach shouted, pointing to the other side of the room. "Here and back."

I squatted and reached out with my arms to the right. I planted my hands — still aching from the bars — and lifted my feet off the ground and kicked to my right. Then I repeated it to my left. We all shuffled, left then right, across the gym floor. It must have looked funny to an outsider. A dozen kids squatting and shuffling like chimps searching for our next meal.

"Don't give up on me now. Cat walk!" Coach yelled. "Backs straight and weight forward."

I shifted from the side-to-side movement to a straight-ahead motion. As my right hand reached out ahead of me, my left foot followed. Then I switched to left hand and right leg. It felt like climbing a ladder laid on the floor. My pace quickened as I loped across the floor and back.

"Who loves crab?"

Coach's jokes were not that funny, especially when it came to training. I turned over so my belly button faced the ceiling. I pushed my hips high and clenched my stomach muscles. My arms reached behind me and I walked like a moving table.

I knew what was coming next. My hands and stomach muscles were not happy about it. We still had bears and frogs left in our intense zoo workout.

"Frog legs, forward *and* backward."

Coach made sure to stress the "and." I guess there would be no breaks today. All the while, I kept thinking how this would pay off in the end. I hoped I was getting stronger. That would make my parkour better.

I squatted, bending my knees deeply. I leaned forward so my hands just touched the mat in front of me. I jumped forward like a frog, kicking my feet out behind me and reaching forward with my hands. I kicked my feet out wide. Then I had to draw them back under the centre of my body.

Everyone was slowing down now. I glanced over to see Parker going slowly. Jayden was just ahead of me. But he was not kicking very high.

The backwards frog was nearly impossible at the end of such a tough training session. I planted my hands, pushed off the mat and kicked my legs back.

"You can't do parkour without muscles!" This was Coach's version of encouragement. He shouted it as he walked alongside us.

He was enjoying watching us suffer, I think. I guess that's what coaches do.

"Last but not least, let me hear you shout it together."

"Beast mode." It was what we called bear walking with a harder twist at the end.

"That's right, ladies and gentlemen. Get your beast walks going. Let's finish strong, shall we?"

I wanted to get it over with. I got down on all fours again. I put my hands out and balanced on my toes. My back was flat. I reached out with my right hand. My left foot followed. We bear walked — left-right, left-right. Then Coach yelled out, "Beast!"

I braced my arms under me and did what looked like a push-up. But one foot — whichever foot you were not using when Coach called out — was suspended in mid-air. The crawling was not so bad. The push-ups were amazingly hard.

My biceps were shaking by the third push-up. At the end of the first line, we turned and headed in the other direction. I reached out with my right hand and lifted my left foot for the first crawl. But before I could get anywhere, my left arm collapsed under me.

I fell on top of it. A shock of pain shot up to my elbow. "Ah!" I cried.

Everyone kept crawling.

Coach came over to me. "Let's see," he said.

I sat up, holding my left wrist with my right hand. I flexed the fingers on my left hand.

"I'm okay," I said.

That was a lie. My wrist was throbbing. But it didn't feel broken. I broke my wrist two years before while skateboarding, so I knew what broken felt like.

"What happened?" he asked me.

"My hand wobbled. I fell on it."

Coach leaned down and put an arm around me. Before I knew it, I was standing.

"Get some ice on that," Coach said as he called an end to practice.

Jayden walked past me as everyone headed for the doors.

"You're getting a lot of attention," he said. "Will getting hurt give you an excuse not to show on demo day?"

I forgot about my wrist. I shook it out and looked back at him. There was no way I was going to let him think I was hurt.

"Nah, I'm fine. Coach was just being nice."

Seriously, would Jayden ever stop? What would parkour be like without Jayden making my life miserable?

15 AS SEEN ON TV

I pulled the note from my pocket. I read it again. I unfolded it and flexed my fingers at the same time. My wrist was almost healed. It only hurt a little when it was bent all the way up or down.

The note was signed by Parker. I found it after my last class, stuffed inside my shoe.

> *Up for an adventure Saturday morning? My mom and I will pick you up at seven o'clock — sharp!*

I tucked the note back in my pocket and pulled out my mom's cell phone. I clicked the button. It said 6:59 a.m. What kind of adventure happens at seven in the morning on a Saturday?

Just as I started wondering if someone — like Jayden — had faked the note, Parker's mom drove up to the curb. The passenger side window rolled down and Parker leaned out.

"Jump in the back!" she called.

Easier said than done. It took some effort to climb up into the back seat. I had to grab hold of the door handle for balance. Their black SUV reminded me of an armoured vehicle.

Parker spun around and handed me a bagel with cream cheese and a bottle of chocolate milk. "Had breakfast yet?" she asked.

"Yeah," I said. "But I can always eat. Where are we going?"

"We're going to be famous," she said, laughing.

She handed me another piece of paper.

"Read it out loud, I want to hear it again."

"Calling all kid actors," I read. "Can you jump, spin or cartwheel? Want to be in a movie? We need fifty kids, ages ten to seventeen, to act as extras in a major motion picture. Gymnastics or martial arts experience needed. Dows Lake Pavilion."

They would provide special clothes. Plus food, soft drinks and an hourly wage. *Food and money?* I thought. *Wicked.*

"Where'd you get this?"

"They sent it to the gymnastics clubs," she said. "My old coach passed it on."

"What's the movie about?"

"I dunno. Maybe it's top secret because of all the big stars!"

We spent the ride guessing who we might see. When the car arrived at the parking lot, we got out, waved goodbye to Parker's mom and jogged across the crosswalk.

A man with a clipboard met us on the other side. "You here to audition?"

"Yeah, we're kid actors," Parker said. "We do parkour."

He looked at us, puzzled. "Okay. Just go down the stairs and around the building. You'll see a room where you hand in your permission slips."

My heart sank. I didn't bring anything.

"Cool," Parker said quickly.

"But . . ." I started to say.

"I have yours here, goofus," she said. "My brother is always forgetting something," she said to the man with a smile.

He stared at us some more, but he didn't say a word. Instead, he just waved his hand for us to keep walking.

"What permission slip?" I asked Parker once we were out of sight.

"Um, I kind of faked yours. I didn't know about the permission slips until late last night. I couldn't have gotten it to you. My mom signed mine before I put my name on it. Then I copied it and wrote your name."

A woman met us in front of the building. She took our signed slips and asked us to wait inside. We sat for probably twenty minutes. Finally, someone came over and handed us some clothes: different pants for Parker and a shirt for me. They applied a little makeup to us both. Then we sat some more.

Finally, the woman from the front of the building came to get us. She pressed a button on her headset. "Hey Zack," she said into it. "I think I have two for you . . . Yup. Yup. Nope. About fourteen, look seventeen. Cute. Yeah? Okay. Great."

She took her finger off the button. My heart was beating faster as she looked back at us.

"You two know how to drive a paddleboat?"

Parker answered before I had a chance to think. "Yes!" she said. "We come here all the time."

"Great, follow me."

We returned outside to a scene of chaos. Three of the crew were carrying cameras. There were silver boxes everywhere. Lights and cables and cameras seemed to burst from the top of them. People running into the building were trying hard not to bump into the people running out of the building.

One guy was running up some stairs, carrying a coil of electrical cable around his shoulder. He passed another guy running down the stairs with what looked like the exact same cable around his shoulder.

"It's a comedy," the woman said.

"I can see that," I said, nodding at the cable guys.

"Huh?" she looked at me and wrinkled her eyebrows.

Parker burst out laughing.

"Oh, yeah," the woman said. I don't think she understood my joke. "Jump into the red paddleboat here. When the director yells action, I need you to kiss for one minute."

"What?" Parker and I shouted at the same time.

"Now who is the comedian?" the woman said.

Parker kept laughing.

"Good one," I said.

"Thanks. So no kiss. But I do need you to sit in the paddleboat. When the director yells action, jump out as fast as you can and run in opposite directions."

"Shouldn't the boat be in the water?" Parker asked.

"Nope, that's what makes it funny. Trust me."

We took our seats. The boat was bolted to the dock. I tried to shake it or move it. But it held firm. A man walked over to us.

"Hey, Zack," I said.

He gave me the same wrinkled eyebrows as the woman had. A funny noise came from Parker as she tried to hold back her laughter.

"Hi," he said.

He crouched down beside us like he was sitting in the boat.

"When I yell 'action,' I need you to lift yourselves out of the boat as fast as you can. Boy runs that way," he said, pointing behind me. "Girl runs that way." He motioned the other way. "Got it?"

"No problem," Parker said.

"Great."

He had us try it a few times. He offered us some

tips on how to make it look funnier. When he was satisfied, he went back to the camera crew.

"I guess we got the part, eh, 'Boy'?" Parker said.

"Looks like it, 'Girl.'"

More people appeared and started buzzing around us. Two people dressed like a bride and groom walked to the end of a dock. We were just behind them, to the left. The cameras were set up and more people appeared. Some carried microphones. Others held smaller cameras.

"Action!"

I jumped from my seat. I turned and started to run. It didn't take long for me to reach the end of that dock area. A metal bar between two posts stood in my way.

Nobody had told me when to stop, so I vaulted over the post and landed on the deck below. I kept running over the boat slips. I had to jump over some water from dock to dock. Finally, I ran out of room on the docks. I jumped back to the main area and vaulted over another metal bar.

There wasn't anywhere else for me to run. Everyone was looking at me.

"Can you do that again?" Zack shouted at me from across the docks.

"Sure," I shouted back.

I looked back at the army of movie makers watching me. *Maybe parkour is useful after all,* I thought.

16 SUPER TRICKY

Our school bus passed signs for horseback riding, cross-country skiing and camping. Finally we pulled into the parking lot of Cloverfield Park.

"Do we have to race the horses?" I asked the kid next to me.

He looked at me with wrinkled eyebrows. People were doing that a lot lately, I realized. I guess if you have to explain your jokes, they are not funny.

"Walk calmly and line up once you get onto the grass," our teacher said. "There are hundreds of kids here. You have your instructions. Don't get lost!"

It was hard to hear her over all of the shouting and laughing. Our bus pulled in next to eight others from schools across the city. More buses were waiting behind ours. I scanned the few faces and buses I could see, looking for the bus from Parker's school. After I'd heard about the race, I'd slipped a flyer inside her shoe at parkour practice.

Super Tricky

On the front was the registration form for School of Hard Knocks, the Ottawa Junior High School Obstacle Course Race. On the back I wrote, *See you at the finish line*. I was pretty sure she'd accept my challenge, especially after we spent Saturday on the movie set.

Our teacher led us to bleachers set up near the start-finish line. My division — for fourteen- and fifteen-year-old boys — was last. It meant I could watch the other kids before running. I climbed the bleachers. Grey clouds had been dropping light rain almost all morning, so I had to be careful. But I wanted to be high enough to see as much as I could and plan my strategy.

The course seemed straightforward. I knew right away my parkour would help. It started with a simple wall. All I needed was enough speed and room. I'd be able to speed vault over it without much trouble. There were some steps on each side. I bet they would be crowded. I planned to stay in the middle to avoid the crowds.

Next was a camouflage net. I would have to crawl on my belly under it. I thought about our beast walks. I hoped my wrist was healed enough.

From there, it was hard to see anything. I could see two A-frame climbing walls, but not in detail. The cross-country running course snaked its way through some trees and bushes. I could only imagine what was waiting for us inside them.

Freerunner

I stood to look at the course behind the bleachers when I spotted a familiar face. Staring up at me was Jayden. He was smirking. I smiled and waved politely. I knew we were about the same age, so I would get my chance to see him up close during the race.

It was an hour before I had to leave for the warm-up area. But all that time I was able to watch and listen. The other schools' kids swirled and whirled around me like birds collecting seeds. They chattered about how heavy the hay bales were to carry. They shared ideas on how to get over the monkey bars. They discussed the best way to crawl under the cargo net. I took it all in.

Sure, this was all just for fun. But I really wanted to win. Especially after seeing Jayden.

The organizers led us in some warm-ups. Then the crowd of boys and girls in my racing group funnelled to the starting area. It felt like we were walking into a gladiator arena. Fences, signs and flags forced us in one direction. There was no turning back. The sun had just started to come out from behind the clouds. Suddenly, everything felt too close, too tight. Boys jostled for space. We lined up six across and maybe ten rows deep. Shoulders bumped easily with nowhere else to turn.

Someone cracked a bad joke: "Mooo. Welcome to the farm!" I was glad it wasn't me, because nobody laughed.

Super Tricky

The girls were grouped ahead of us. Just before they started, I spotted Parker. She was too far away and there were too many people between us for me to wish her good luck. I memorized her orange T-shirt and knew I'd see her after the race.

Finally, it was our turn. I ran through in my mind what I knew of the course. I decided there was no point trying to get out first. It was a long race — the fastest time so far was twenty-eight minutes or so. There would be plenty of time to catch the leaders. I had to pace myself. I had to be smart about the obstacles.

The horn sounded. We were off and running. Jayden and his buddies bolted like race horses for the first obstacle. I let a few keeners skip ahead of me. I wanted my space to vault the wall.

Just like I had guessed, most kids ran for the steps. The middle was wide open. So I took the space, placed my hands on top of the wall and kicked my legs over. I must have passed twelve kids that way. They were all crowded in a line waiting for the stairs. Some of them looked at me as if to say, *I didn't know we could do it that way!*

Next were yellow plastic tunnels snaking along the ground. After that, off to the right, were hay bales. It was another great chance to use some parkour and gain some time. I chose the tunnel farthest to the right. I wanted to have the best route to the bales.

The tunnels were coiled together. My hands and knees didn't enjoy skimming over the edges. My wrists hurt a little from the hard plastic. I'd already caught up to one of Jayden's buddies, though. He was one who had been sprinting from the start. I guess he didn't have the endurance after all.

It was slow, following him through the tunnel. I managed to get some room around him, even though it seemed like he was trying hard to nudge me off the course. I took two big steps ahead and he couldn't follow.

The hay bales were the perfect size. I put both hands ahead of me and pounced. My legs swung underneath and I vaulted past another few competitors. That obstacle was made for the Kong vault.

"Whoa! Awesome!" someone shouted behind me.

That gave me a burst of confidence. I kept running.

17 BOSS BATTLE

The race got flatter, slower and heavier. The obstacles seemed to vanish. So did my parkour. I was running ahead of about eight others. We rounded some trees to find what looked like an arena. It was separated by fences from the race course.

There were a few kids already carrying straw bales. "What the hay?" I said.

It was too bad nobody was around to hear my joke.

"You'll pair with the racer behind you," the marshal said. "It's teamwork time."

I had no idea who the kid behind me was. Each bale was wrapped with a thick strap. I grabbed one end and a sturdy-looking kid in a purple T-shirt grabbed the other. We carried it along the fence. Then we swung it across a line marked in the dirt, where it landed with the other hay bales in a cloud of dust.

We shuffled down a small hill where another challenge awaited us. Racers were rolling big tractor tires from one end of a yard to the other and back.

"Okay, now I'm tired," I said.

The kid in the purple T-shirt gave me a look.

I bent at the knees, dug my hands under the tire and lifted. The tire was as tall as me. But it wasn't too heavy. I immediately thought about home. My uncle had wanted to pay me twenty dollars a day to help him sort through junker cars. I must have had something better to do. Or maybe it was too much work, because I only did it once. Now I wish I had stuck it out.

I started rolling the tire. It wobbled right away and nearly fell. I sped up and it rolled much smoother. But then it got away from me and fell on its side, off the course. I ran up behind it and bent to grab it again. By the time I finally got it up and finished rolling it back, I had lost precious time.

I'd thought Jayden was in the arena with me. But now I could see his neon green shirt jumping over an A-frame on the other side of the course.

I really had to pick up the pace. The A-frames had knobs drilled into them like a rock-climbing wall. I ran ahead of two kids to get the best path over it. I skipped the knobs and instead jumped for the top of the frame. My feet landed first and I grabbed the top with my hands. I had cleared the bottom half of it with one swoop.

Precision jumps were moves we worked on at the gym all the time.

Once I pulled my body to the top, it wasn't that far

down. So I leaped forward, ducked and landed with a parkour roll. It spun me forward and I was sprinting hard for the next challenge.

My heart was beating hard in my chest now. Spread out ahead of us was a cargo net about half a metre off the ground. We had to crawl under it, army style. It was time for "beast mode." I dove down so my belly was close to the ground. I alternated right arm, left leg with right leg and left arm. I crawled ten metres, keeping as low as possible for a fast time.

It was nothing compared to Coach's workouts.

Jayden was just scrambling out as I started the cargo crawl. I knew it would be a close finish. When I stood up again, it was just me and him. There was a monkey-bar set between us and the finish line.

From what I could see, there were two options. You could swing across the bars, like the laché bars at the gym. But there had to be a dozen of them. My arms were throbbing as I approached. There was no way I could swing across very fast. Plus, there was a mud pit down below. If I fell into that, winning would be almost impossible.

There were rock-climbing pegs on the outside of the monkey bars along a wood frame. That meant you could shimmy along the outside beams. There wouldn't be any mud to worry about. But you'd need an amazing grip. That way might be even slower than the bars.

I stopped for a second. Jayden glanced back at me. He stopped too, leaning over to catch his breath. We watched another kid sprint past us. He jumped for the first bar and started to swing. He made it across three of them before losing his grip and splatting into the mud. His legs and feet were covered in it. He had to drag himself out and try again.

Jayden took off after that. He was making good time on the bars when I spotted something. The wood beams holding the bars were thick. There were two ways across the mud. Could there be a third?

I decided to risk it. I went to the side and stepped on the first peg. I grabbed two more and climbed to the top. The beams were as wide as they looked from the ground. Rather than standing, I crouched and walked like a cat along the top of the beam.

In seconds, I was ahead of Jayden. His face was red and his knuckles were white. He could only hang there and watch me from the middle of the bars.

As I slipped past him, I heard a roar. All the earlier racers, teachers and organizers were watching from the finish line. They were cheering. I reached the end of the beam, grabbed the last bar and started to swing. Once my body was almost horizontal, I let go and went sailing. I landed and did another parkour roll just for fun. I jogged across the finish line alone.

Parker ran up to me and gave me a hug. Kids from my school who'd barely known my name before were patting me on the back.

Organizers put a medal around my neck. Jayden must have found the strength from somewhere, because he finished second just a minute later. Parker and I were there to congratulate him. I couldn't see any point in staying angry at him.

"That move at the end was impressive, Tricky," he said.

I wasn't expecting that. It sounded like a compliment. "Thanks."

"It's funny that nobody else thought of it."

I guess he thought it was cheating. That's more of what I expected from him. "You know the medals are all the same," I said. "They all say 'finisher.' There's no first or second."

The crowds and the race organizers forced us all to shuffle forward. There was an awkward silence as Jayden and I stood shoulder to shoulder.

"True," he said. "And I don't really care about this. We will see how the demo day goes. That's what I'm worried about."

My head spun around when he said that. He was worried about something. Was it his performance or mine?

"I'll be there," I said. "But I'm not really worried about it."

I think Jayden realized what he had admitted to. He changed the subject.

"Coach won't let you quit parkour, will he? It's almost like he knows you. You know, from work. Ever run into him when he's wearing a uniform? Maybe that's why you're at the gym all the time. So he can keep an eye on you."

I knew he was bluffing. Coach promised me he would never tell anyone why I was taking parkour. But it made me happy that Jayden had stopped smirking. He was worried and thinking of ways to take me down. He was taking me seriously.

18 BREAKING "THE BANK"

I stepped off the bus and shielded my eyes from the blazing Sunday morning sunshine. A block ahead I could see the Bank. It looked empty, which was perfect. I didn't want anyone watching me. I wanted to try some things without anyone chasing me off for running along the walls or vaulting the statues.

Parker had invited me to train with her there exactly two months before. I barely knew anything then. My vaults were slow and shaky. Every so often, I'd hurt my back on a parkour roll. Now, everything was quicker and smoother. Nothing hurt — very much, anyway. And I wasn't scared to try the moves outside the gym.

I crossed the empty street and approached the Bank from behind the tall trees. A familiar voice echoed ahead of me. I ducked under some low-hanging branches. I peered from behind the tree and just about barfed. There, running the walls, were Jayden and Parker. I felt like someone had punched me in the stomach.

I was pretty sure they couldn't see me, so I sat down. I didn't want to watch them. But I couldn't turn away. They were having fun.

Laughter echoed around me. Jayden was flying over the statues. He was running over the Maritimes in a side-step pattern. I had never thought of that. It made total sense. I kind of hated him for thinking of it.

Parker vaulted over Saskatchewan and ran through the dry fountain. She curled back again and vaulted Manitoba.

I considered stepping out of the trees and breaking up their fun. I was angry. Just a few days before, Parker had been hugging me at the finish line of the obstacle course. Now, she was with a guy who had tried to get me kicked out of the club.

I flexed my legs under me. But I didn't stand. Soon Healthy Habits Day would be done and I would be free. I would never have to see Parker or Jayden again. If I confronted Jayden, who knows what would happen. Maybe I'd end up back in court. Instead, I decided to sneak away.

I must have walked for twenty minutes. But I wasn't getting anywhere. I was surrounded by concrete buildings and freeways. I was trying to get near the water. But the best park was back where I'd just come from. I'd come downtown to practise.

Forget it, I thought. *I'm going back. I don't care if something happens.*

Breaking "the Bank"

As I appeared through the trees, Parker stopped running and stared. Jayden was on top of Quebec. He turned to look at me. But he didn't wave. And he didn't jump off the statue.

"Hey," I said.

Parker's face started to turn red. And it wasn't from running. I think she was embarrassed. I was having a hard time hiding my anger. She could probably see that too.

"I thought you were security or something," she said. "Hey, you wanna trace with us?"

I looked at Jayden. He turned and headed toward the Maritimes. I guess he didn't care.

"Yeah, I guess," I said.

I ran at Manitoba and jumped on top of it as Jayden jumped off the last statue. I leaped over the gap to Ontario and then to Quebec. Parker joined behind me. I stepped across to New Brunswick, dancing between Nova Scotia, Prince Edward Island and Newfoundland and Labrador.

My feet were light, never resting on any surface for more than a second. My balance was low. My knees were flexed as I looked ahead for the next place to land.

I jumped off into a parkour roll. Parker followed me. Jayden drifted off to the trees and some shade. He watched for a while. Parker and I kept circling through.

"My turn to lead," she shouted.

I followed her back the other way and we reversed the course. After fifteen minutes, we were both wiping away sweat. Jayden just sat and watched. Parker finally waved me over to where Jayden was sitting. She bent to get a water bottle. I followed, keeping her between Jayden and me. She offered me her bottle. I gratefully accepted.

"It's cool you showed up," she said.

I thought about that for a minute. Most of my anger was gone. Parkour had that effect on me. Parkour was better with other people. I was learning just by watching how other people approached obstacles.

"Yeah, I just want to be ready for next week."

"Us too," Parker said.

Us? I thought. *Why did she say, 'us'? Are she and Jayden an 'us' now?*

I wanted to know why they were here. I just didn't know how to ask. I was also hurt. If I was back in Red Rock, I would have kept walking. I would have given up on Parker. I would have told myself she wasn't worth it. But that was a long time ago. And Parker was important to me. At least I thought she was, until I saw her here. Maybe I didn't know her well enough. Maybe I should stick around and get to know her better.

"I guess this is the best place to train," I said, finally.

"For sure," Parker said quickly. "I used to come here with Jayden every week, before . . ."

She didn't finish her sentence. Jayden looked up at me. She was going to say they came here more before I showed up at the gym. Jayden stood. He grabbed his water bottle and checked his phone.

"Our ride is coming," he said.

He started walking away. But he stopped and turned back after only a couple of steps.

"You got pretty good at this," Jayden said, looking right at me. "I guess I'll have to be on my toes at the demo." And then he kept walking.

He was being nice to me. Well, as nice as possible for him. Now I was really confused. My eyes glanced at Parker. But they didn't stay for very long.

"You okay?" she asked me.

"Yeah, sure."

She hoisted her backpack onto her shoulder and stared at me. I couldn't look her in the eye.

"It doesn't mean anything, Tricky. Jayden and me being here," she said.

"Jayden hates me," I replied, quieter this time. "But I thought you liked me."

"I do," she said. "Okay, look, I'm sorry. Jayden asked me. I knew you wouldn't come with us. Plus, that would be weird."

"So you decided to sneak around?"

"I didn't sneak," she said. "Jayden and I have known each other a long time. He and his friends are all spoiled rich kids. He likes hanging out with me because I don't care about his shoes or his haircut. That's why I like you too. Because you don't care about your shoes or your haircut."

My head was spinning. Finally, I realized it was up to me. I had to trust that Parker was telling me the truth. And I did, even as she hugged me goodbye and left with Jayden. What I didn't know was if it was enough.

19 DEMO DAY

We piled out of Coach's van at the Healthy Habits Day event. Four young boys playing "ninjas" nearly crashed into us. One kid spotted our black–and–yellow T-shirts.

"Cool, you do parkour?" he said.

"Yeah, you should come watch us," I replied.

In just a few hours, this whole thing would be done. My demo would be finished. I'd be free. I looked up at the sprawling lawn filled with hundreds of people.

"Let's go take a look at the course," Parker said. "I can't wait!"

We moved through a crush of kids and their parents, all checking out the various sporting booths and areas. They were trying everything from ballet to boxing. First were boys shooting pucks on artificial ice. Next to that, young kids were dancing a hip hop routine. Beyond them, girls watched a friend pull a bowstring to fire an arrow at a red-and-blue hay bale target.

"I have to come back and try that," Parker said.

I looked at her and smiled. I was still trying to figure out what had happened the weekend before.

"Last week, I'm glad you told me what you did," I said. "And I know I haven't said much to you. But I have something I need to say now."

"Wait, me first," she interrupted. "When I saw you with those kids at the gym, I knew you weren't like Jayden. I'm really glad you joined parkour. I like you and I like Jayden. But it's different. Hey, remember, I faked your signature for that movie thing. I wouldn't do that for just anyone."

I wasn't sure that made what I was going to tell her any easier.

"My turn," I said. "Parker, I'm not here because I want to be. Coach, he caught me shoplifting. But he said if I did parkour for three months, I wouldn't get in trouble. This is the last day. So you won't have to see me at the gym anymore. I'm pretty sure you won't want to hang out with me after hearing about the shoplifting, though, and that's cool. I understand."

Parker stopped. Before she could answer, a crowd of little kids ran between us. I was okay with that. It felt good just to get it off my chest. But I wasn't sure how she was going to react.

I didn't have much time to think about it, either. The parkour set-up was at the centre of the park. It distracted us both.

Demo Day

It was amazing. There were bars with rings hanging down. Three sizes of vault ran down the middle. A wall that had to be five metres high towered over the far end. It was curved and had the word "Warped!" spray-painted through the middle like a tag. On the far side were stairs to a platform. Below that were walls with cut-out windows and doors. They had horizontal bars across the frame or across the corners. There were boxes with angled tops along the ground and two sets of rails. It was up to us to decide how to use it all. We could make up our own routines.

Our team stopped along the fence. Nobody said anything for a while.

"Whoa, whoever did this is really awesome," Jayden said finally.

I had to agree. More teams started arriving and we got ready to warm up. Before long, the place was buzzing. Electronic dance music bounced from the speakers. After about fifteen minutes, an announcer on a loudspeaker asked us to get ready to start the demo.

We watched as the first three teams ran through their routines. There were some really cool moves, even from the younger kids. A nine-year-old girl named Isobel got the biggest applause when she breezed through the rings into a spinning dismount.

Parker went first for our team. Her routine was heavy on gymnastics. She used cartwheels, back handsprings and front twists. She vaulted over the boxes in the centre and swung under the handrails.

She ended on the top vault. Instead of going over it, though, she jumped onto it. She leaned forward, placed her hands on the top, and stretched into a handstand. She held it there for a few seconds, giving the crowd a chance to cheer.

Then she kicked her legs forward to flip onto the ground.

"Yeah, Parker!" I shouted.

Everyone on our team stood and clapped.

It gave me a burst of energy for my turn. I jumped to my feet and ran to the end of the course. I took a deep breath and rocked back on my heels. Then I leaned forward and bolted for the first vault. I put my hand onto the vault and kicked over with my legs. I started with a thief vault.

It was the only kind of thief I wanted to be known as now.

My legs pushed me for the Warped Wall. I slammed my right foot hard into the bottom of the ramp and kicked with my left.

I took two more steps on the ramp before I stretched. My left hand reached the ledge first. My right hand darted from my side and I grabbed hold. I let go, spun and headed down the wall.

The curved base gave me the momentum I needed. I ran for the laché bars, jumping high to grab the first.

My legs swung easily forward. The momentum shot me higher and I grabbed the second horizontal bar.

I kept swinging, kicking my legs high and twisting my body so I spun 180 degrees. That slowed me down, though. My body felt heavy, so I swung my legs twice to regain some power.

I managed to generate enough thrust to get to the next bar. My arms were tight. I needed to use my legs instead. My plan was to do something nobody had thought of during the practice time.

I dashed through the open "door" cut from the wooden frame. To be cute, I turned and waved goodbye. There was room back there to hide from the crowd. I heard laughter and some clapping.

I found open space that led directly to a "window." Waiting for a beat in the music, I started my run along the path. Just as the drums exploded — *bap, bap, bap* . . . *BOOM* — I burst through the window into a parkour roll. The crowd erupted again.

I headed for the next vault. I stretched out my arms, planted both hands and dragged my legs through for a Kong vault. It was the farthest I had ever vaulted in my life. I stood and stretched my arms up to the sky just as the music stopped with an explosion of drums. It was luck, for sure. But it was perfect. The fans must have thought I was a genius, as they roared their approval.

There were so many emotions running through me, I couldn't tell what was strongest. It had been twelve weeks since the whole mess had started. I couldn't believe I was able to pull off this routine. I was amazed at how the crowd and other teams were there to help me through.

It was enough. I was happy. I walked back to where I'd left my bag on the grass. Parker and Coach watched me as I neared them. I peeled the tape from my fingers and tossed it into the garbage. On the other side of the fence was my freedom. I picked up my bag and looked at the gate.

20 RISING AND FALLING

As I lifted my backpack over my shoulder, I turned and looked back at the course. Parker was running up to me. She hugged me before I could move any farther.

"That was amazing," she said. "Where are you going? You look like you're leaving. But you have to stay with me, with the team."

"Okay," I said. "I wasn't going anywhere, honest."

"We have to celebrate tonight, in the market. It's my treat. I might even let you have your own dessert."

"Really? Are your friends coming?"

"No, they aren't invited. It's just you and me."

I don't think I'd ever been happier.

"Deal," I said.

We turned as Jayden stood to start his run.

Parker and I sat down next to Coach in the athletes' area along the barricades. The music started again and butterflies hit my stomach. I did want him to do well, even after all that had happened.

He bent at the waist, dipped his head and swung his legs around. It was one of his usual martial arts moves, a butterfly twist. Then he took a big step with his right foot and another with his left foot. His right foot kicked around him and he spun in midair, nearly horizontal, for a corkscrew jump.

His next jump started the same way, with two big steps, left and right. Off his left foot, he jumped back and kicked his right leg hard. It spun him around for what looked like a backflip, or at least half of a backflip.

"What do you call that?" I whispered to Parker.

"He calls it a cheat gainer," she said. "He learned it on YouTube."

"It looks kind of cool."

"Yeah, I could teach you in five minutes."

"Okay," I said. "I'd like that."

She smiled at me. Suddenly, I didn't feel the need to run away anymore.

Jayden was making his way for the Warped Wall. He ran up to the top ledge and pulled himself up. Then he jumped off the top, and down into a parkour roll. He stood and ran for the rings.

His approach seemed fast to me. He extended his hand for the first ring. But he slipped off, falling awkwardly onto his side.

"Oh!" the crowd gasped.

Jayden stood quickly. I thought he might have hurt his shoulder. And he looked confused. He stepped away from the rings and headed again for the Warped Wall. He planted his right foot and spun around it, going for another twisting jump. He was too close and too slow, though. He stumbled into a landing.

Now I was starting to feel really bad for him.

"Yeah, let's go Jayden!" Parker yelled. We started to clap together.

"Give it all you've got, Jayden!" Coach yelled.

He headed for the Wall again, dive rolling through the cut-out window just like I had done.

"That was good," I said. "He's okay now, I think."

"I hope so," Parker said. "He's been going for a long time. He might be getting tired."

Jayden was lined up for the vaults. He used speed vaults over the first, then safety vaults over the next two. He faced the Warped Wall again. *He's in the right spot at least*, I thought. *But he's going to need all his strength.*

Jayden started his approach. He got two good plants and jumped for the top. He caught the ledge and hauled himself up with both hands.

"Whoa, now what?" Parker asked. "There's no way he has anything left."

Jayden was standing on top of the wall, five metres in the air. The crowd perked up. People in the audience clapped and whistled. Jayden looked like he was deciding what to do next.

"I really hope he doesn't try anything dumb," I said.

He walked toward the edge and looked down.

"Whatever you're thinking, Jayden, don't do it," Parker muttered. "Just sit down, please."

The music was too loud for him to hear us. I think Parker was hoping Jayden would get some kind of psychic message. She put her hands over her ears and closed her eyes. I stretched my neck to watch. Jayden was almost above where we were sitting. I couldn't turn away.

The crowd started to clap rhythmically. They expected a big finish. Coach was trying to calm down Jayden by waving his hands slowly.

"Just come down, Jay," Coach yelled up.

That seemed to work. Jayden turned backward to ease himself down. I could see his chest heaving. He looked tired. He was also too close to the edge. His foot slipped. He caught himself just enough. But now half his body was dangling off the side of the ledge. In an instant, he lost his grip and started to slide on his belly over the edge.

Someone in the crowd shrieked.

I jumped to my feet. We were close and I was able to help him down as he slid awkwardly down the wall. He regained his balance and turned around to see me there.

"Tricky, thanks," he said.

"Yeah, no problem. You okay?"

"I'm fine."

His face was bright red. The crowd was clapping again. Coach and Parker were behind me. Coach hoisted Jayden down from his awkward perch. We all headed back to our seats.

Jayden turned to face me directly. He extended his arm. I grabbed it and we shook hands. I wasn't sure it made up for the past three months. But I didn't want our rivalry to keep going, either.

I led the way as our team walked out of the parkour demo area.

"That was intense," Jayden said to Parker and me. "How about tomorrow we trace at the Bank together? I need to work on some stuff."

From the corner of my eye, I could see that Coach was listening.

"I have a better idea," I said. "I know some great spots near the art gallery beside the Rideau Centre."

Coach looked right at me and laughed.

"Just don't get into any trouble," he said.

Parker grinned. Jayden looked a little confused at first. But I think he figured it out pretty quickly.

"Nah," I said. "I've learned my lesson."

ACKNOWLEDGEMENTS

Special thanks first go to coach Dagan Shaw at DShawPK in Ottawa for his insights into teaching young people about parkour. Also, thank you to coach Ivan Gorbenko and his adult parkour class at Kelowna Gymnastix. As always, special thanks to editor Kat Mototsune and everyone at Lorimer for their guidance and support.